give
it to
the grand
canyon

noah cicero

Published by Philosophical Idiot
Phillipsburg, NJ
www.philosophicalidiot.com

Cover art: "Kop can een koningsgier of condor
(Gypagus Papa)" by M.E. van den Brink Bequest, Velp

Cover design by Olivia M. Croom
(oliviacroomdesign.com)

Author photo by Sam Dee.

Portions of this book have been published
by *The Nervous Breakdown, New York Tyrant,*
& Philosophical Idiot.

IBSN-13: 9781732292215
ISBN-10: 1732292213

Arrival at the Canyon

1.

"Give it to the Grand Canyon," that's what she said to me.

The first time I went to the Grand Canyon was when I was 12 years old. It was 1992—Nirvana, Pearl Jam and En Vogue. My father bought an old '70s Winnebago, it was ugly and the toilet barely worked. My father said, "We are going to drive this to California and then throw it away." He knew the score on that vehicle, its time was short, but it had some life left in it, it had one more trip.

I grew up in Ohio, a flat land of trees, steel mills, whitetail deer, muddy trails through forested lands. I walked cornfields in the summer and stood in three feet of snow in the winter. I had never seen a mountain or a cactus, I had never seen The West, had never known a dust devil or the great mountains of Colorado. I had never seen the great big skies, the panoramas that had no end.

I was a 12-year-old boy. My father, brother and I went across America in the Winnebago. I looked out the window at the cornfields of Nebraska and Kansas. Where did all the corn come from, where was it going to go? How did the world make so much corn?

Then we went to the Salt Flats of the Nevada/Utah border, a vista of salt and mountains with no trees. We drove out to the mountains, there wasn't anything there but heat, dust and cacti. It wasn't like a movie, it was real, the desert was there, and I was there, and we were together. I loved it and wanted more of it.

In Las Vegas, when we stayed at the Circus, it was 116 degrees that day. It felt like heat from an oven, my body liked it. Saw grandma in California, went swimming in LA, saw a dead seal on the beach. Grandma had a tangerine tree in her yard.

Eventually the Winnebago was pointed back to Ohio, there was only one step left, one last destination, the Grand Canyon. I don't think I even cared at that point, I was young and didn't care about a giant hole. It was my father and brother that cared so much.

We took a left off I-40 onto 60 and then to 180, and drove the hour and a half north. I don't remember the drive north, but it must have happened. We arrived at the South Rim. We all went to the edge in front of the Bright Angel Restaurant and there it was, the Grand Canyon. I don't remember seeing it exactly, but the feeling was strong, the feeling of experiencing it was powerful, overwhelming, some sort of answer I was always looking for. There it was, it didn't look real, so many colors, so many cracks, so much imprecision. It was a war against civilization. Civilization is efficient, things are perfect and mathematical, the curves of civilization are beautiful, the lines are straight. In civilization time is everything, tomorrow at 7am you better be at school, math class starts at 10:20am. But the Grand Canyon had no concern for time, it had no concern for straight lines or perfect curves.

The Grand Canyon was not produced by a steel mill or a car factory, it was created by something else, something more powerful, something less concerned with making money and owning nice clothes.

Then we went to the Desert View Tower. We went into the souvenir shop and my brother bought a funny cowboy-looking hat. He wore it a few times when he got back to Ohio, soon after he abandoned it, I kept it in my closet to remember the trip, I would look at it and smile. The hat is gone now.

I watched the sunset at Desert View in 1992. It was like all my American dreams had come true. They had never come true in Ohio, but there in Arizona, they had come true. I don't know why I felt so attracted to the Grand Canyon, what was inside me, or what was inside it, that compelled me to such emotion, but I knew it was *true*.

The next time I ended up at The Grand Canyon it was 2000, eight years had passed, but I never forgot what I felt there. I would daydream of the Canyon at school, before I went to bed at night, when I was driving my car. There it was, the Canyon, in my mind.

I was near the end of my senior year of high school, and I wanted to see the world, I couldn't contain myself, I was starting college in the fall and didn't want spend that summer doing what I had done the previous 18 years of my life, sitting around drinking beers around bonfires, basically doing nothing, I had to get on the road. I went on the Internet and found a website for jobs at the Grand Canyon, printed out the application and sent it across America. It was the first document I ever sent by mail, and I felt really proud of myself. The Grand Canyon called me on the phone, someone told me I was hired to wash dishes at the El Tovar. I didn't know what an El Tovar was, but it seemed fine.

I graduated high school on a Friday. Sunday morning I was on the road to the Grand Canyon. I was an 18-year-old boy who had decided to leave his home, I didn't have one friend with me. I was totally alone in a 1989 Caprice Classic, a big V8, flying down the highway smoking cigarettes, drinking Gatorade and eating beef jerky. It rained and stormed all day until I got to the arches of St. Louis. The sky cleared, blue skies, for the rest of the drive.

Somewhere in Nebraska I was pooping in a bathroom and saw written on the wall of the stall, "Lost in America." I knew that was my fate.

In the Colorado Rockies, I believe it was Georgetown, I was sitting on the roof of my car eating McDonald's, and there they were, the Rockies. Mountains and mountains, mountains that demanded expertise to get to the top, not little West Virginia hills, but real monsters, real Gods towering over the landscape. The air was clean and felt soft on the skin, the sky a light blue. I was alone at the top of the world, at the top of America.

When I arrived at The Grand Canyon they gave me a room in Victor Hall, or Victim Hall as some called it. I was introduced to people from all over the world immediately, I was a small-town boy, I wasn't ready for that. The Grand Canyon had an international program that brought students from France, Costa Rica, Korea and other places I can no longer remember. I remember washing dishes with two Korean kids who loved Bon Jovi, and talking on the stone porch of Victor Hall with crazy French guys who had read Proust and Victor Hugo.

I also met Native Americans for the first time. There are none left in Ohio. I met Hopis and Navajos. I sat in the TV room till 3am listening to Navajos tell me stories about how their language came from rabbits and how they fought in Vietnam. But I got fired from the Grand Canyon for drinking on the job. I was changing the garbage at the bar and the bartender, a long-haired white boy, a real '90s kid, said, "I have a shot no one wanted, you want to drink it?" I looked around and saw only one person at the bar, a middle-aged woman that looked like a tourist. I was like, "Okay," and drank the shot. About 20 minutes later I was called in the office, my young 18-year-old self was called to sit in front of the manager in some weird makeshift office. The boss told me I was fired. I had failed, I was fired, stupid stupid self, what did you do? You took a stupid shot and ruined everything. I signed a paper saying I quit peacefully and left the office. I told my buddies in the dishtank, "I just got fired for drinking." They all looked shocked, but it was normal for Victor Hall Midwest boys to get fired for drinking.

When I told my friend Charlie what happened, we decided we'd go to California next. Charlie wanted to leave the canyon. There was something I had to do before I could leave, I had to hike to the bottom. I wanted to get to that bottom, where the Colorado River swirled and whooshed.

Charlie was this funny guy from New Zealand, he was traveling the world, he had traveled around America and lived in Costa Rica. He had a woman in Costa Rica, her name was Leonora. Charlie would call her on the phone and send her emails from the computers at the recreation center. But Charlie never returned to Costa Rica and Leonora married someone else and had kids. Charlie got a law degree and now lives in New York City as a musician.

Charlie and I made it to the bottom, it was shimmering green. Only those who have been to the bottom of The Grand Canyon know what "shimmering green" means, yes, it shimmers green.

On our way back up Bright Angel Trail, the sun set on us and our feet started to hurt. Charlie and I didn't know anything about hiking. We just wore normal sneakers, we didn't have cool backpacks, protein bars or REI made pants. We had our old school packs and Chex Mix. Blisters swelled in our shoes, one the size of a quarter formed on my left heel. We could barely walk, but we knew we had to get to the top of the canyon. We had to leave for California the next afternoon. We had a mission, we knew it was true and had to be done.

As we slowly hiked up Bright Angel it began to drizzle. We had no ponchos, we let it rain on us. We didn't have flashlights, the moon lit our way. As we were walking through the darkness a Navajo came out of nowhere, like some kind of weird dream. The middle-aged Navajo said in his native accent, "You seen my sister?" And we replied, "No, we aren't sure." Then the man kept walking.

When we made it to the top, it was night, and all the cafeterias were closed, but we were starving. We got in my Caprice and drove down to Tusayan and got ourselves some cheeseburgers from McDonald's.

In 2006, when I was 25, I went with a woman I was dating, her name was Leslie. We drove across America together, from Ohio to the California coast. We stopped in the Rockies but that time I slept in the National Park. We hiked a mountain until a mountain lion scared us back down the hill. Then we went through Nevada. We skipped Las Vegas and drove up the Extraterrestrial Highway in the middle of the night. It was the longest night of our lives, jackrabbits dashing across the road, they were everywhere, we must have killed ten that night. Where did all those jackrabbits come from? Aren't coyotes supposed to eat them?

There wasn't one place to sleep that long night in Nevada. We stopped in Caliente, but there were no rooms and a cop yelled at us, "Slow down, this is Cal ee an ee." The Spanish pronunciation had disappeared and so had the T. We walked into a bar and felt scared, everyone looked like strange desert people, like they had come from the same holes and darkness as the jackrabbits.

After Nevada we went to Los Angeles to Disneyland, then to San Diego and Tijuana. On the way back we stopped at the Grand Canyon. I showed Leslie the park, I showed her Victor Hall, and we took a bus and looked at some points. We didn't stay long, but there it was, the Grand Canyon.

I didn't see the Grand Canyon again until 2013, eight years had passed. Since then, I've gone to the North Rim and the Skywalk. I believe I am a true aficionado of that canyon. Here is my story of what happened in the summer of 2013, after I returned from living three years in South Korea as an ESL teacher.

2.

It doesn't matter why I decided to go to live at the Grand Canyon, why a 33-year-old man isn't married, doesn't have kids or a career. When I look at Facebook at the people I graduated with, I can see they have settled down. They found a place to live in this world. Most live within thirty miles of their parents, a few went to North Carolina, a couple went out west, but most live near home. Then there was me, I lived in South Korea, and not for a year, but three. I couldn't go home, they paid me well and gave me free rent. I would go out on the weekends in Seoul, I would go to Itaewon and Hongdea, and party all night, the parties of my dreams. Thousands of people in the street, so many voices, so much joy, lovers fighting, marines fighting, and everyone too drunk. It felt really special at those places, on those nights, it felt good to be surrounded by so many with a singular purpose.

But the party ended, I woke up one day and knew I had to go back home. I fought it at first, I told myself I was still excited to be there, but I wasn't. I didn't know what I was doing. When my contract ended, I took a plane home. But when I returned, everything was changed. My friends didn't know me anymore, and I didn't know them. Their lives had changed, they had new jobs, they had gotten married, had kids, bought houses. They had watched major sporting events together, they had grown up, and I had missed it. A lot of important things had happened in their lives, and I had missed all of it. And what made it worse, when I got home, I wasn't thinking about anything but myself. I seriously thought everyone wanted to hear my stories, I kept saying, "In Korea they do this." I realized I had become really annoying.

When I looked around my hometown, there was nothing there that spoke to me. Even my parents seemed far away, everything they said fell flat and meaningless. We were never close, but after two years of being away for grad school and three years of being away, there was nothing left.

I took a plane to Flagstaff, the town 90 miles south of the Grand Canyon, the closest outpost where people can get cheap groceries and new clothes and have a fun night out without being surrounded by tourists.

I stayed at the Motel Dubeau, a cheap hostel. I got a bed in a room full of beds, several were bunk beds. I picked out a bed in the corner, put down my bag and changed my clothes. What was I doing in a hostel? 30-something-year-old men don't sleep in dorms, they sleep in hotels. After I changed I went to a brewery across the street, I sat at the bar, it wasn't an attractive bar, just a nice room for people to sit. I had thousands of dollars leftover from Korea, buying a meal wouldn't matter. I ordered an IPA and a sandwich. What was I doing there? I had no place to go, I had lost all my friends to time. No one spoke to me at the bar. Everyone looked a million miles away, they were people who had friends and families and they believed in romance and entanglements. It wasn't that I didn't believe in entanglements, I'd just forgotten how to have them.

I went back to the hostel, the room was dark, travelers were sleeping in their beds. I went to my corner, put on my sleepy clothes, went to the bathroom and brushed my teeth.

3.

My alarm woke me up, I had to get ready and be at the train station at 7am to get on the bus that would take me to the Grand Canyon. I went to the shower, shaved my face, prepared myself. It felt like I was meeting an old friend, and I needed to look good for this meeting.

There was breakfast in the hostel, I poured a cup of coffee and got some waffles. There were other people outside, mostly from other countries. I didn't know them and they didn't know me. We didn't talk. I had nothing to say to anyone. I drank my coffee while the sun slowly lit up Flagstaff.

I put my bag together and headed out the door. The clerk told me to walk straight up the street and there would be the train station. I pulled my red luggage down the road, over the train tracks. The sun still had not completely risen.

When I got to the station, there were a few others waiting. There were two Bulgarian young women in their early 20s, both beautiful. One was a skinny blonde with blue eyes, and the other was a stronger, darker-looking woman. The little blonde spoke to me, she told me her name was Boyona, I said my name is Billy. I felt maybe I would have felt sexually attracted to her and tried to flirt, but I didn't care, I felt no enthusiasm concerning flirting. It was too early in the morning to laugh.

She told me she was from Bulgaria, that it was her second summer at the Grand Canyon. That she was going to be a cashier in the Maswick cafeteria. Her friend was going to work at the El Tovar hotel as a boss. She asked me what I was going to do. I said I was going to work as a cashier in the Bright Angel restaurants. I didn't ask her about Bulgaria.

A good-sized van came with ten seats and no bathroom. I felt scared of having to go to the bathroom. Would I make it 73 miles without having to go to the bathroom?

The bus took us down the highway 180. I looked out the window, there was nothing, some trees, but mostly nothing. I had spent the first 24 years of my life in tree-filled Ohio. If you didn't cut the grass and maintain the landscape, trees were soon to come. The trees lined up on the sides of the highways like armies ready to march onto the cement as soon as humans died and went away. I could always hear the trees say in Ohio, "For thousands of years we have lived here doing whatever we want, growing here growing there, but then you came. You cut us down, killed our sprouts before they could grow. And when you die and go away, we will return and claim this land as ours."

When I was little, I never wanted to be in the house. It was a small house and the television was perpetually on. When my father woke up at 5am he would go into the living room and turn on the television. He would drink coffee watching the morning news, in silence. Then my older brothers would wake up and watch television with him. Then we would all go to school or work. When I returned home from school the television was on, at eight we would gather around the television in silence. No one ever talked, the television talked for us. We listened. The television told us true things, and we obeyed. At eleven my father would watch the news, I knew the news anchors like family members, I would eventually go to sleep. My mother would come home from the factory around midnight, drop her

16

huge chain of keys on the kitchen table, then sit down and watch television until 2am. The television was never off, no one ever talked.

I became obsessed with the forest behind my house. Every time I got a chance I would walk the old dirt bike trails. When I grew tired of the trails, I started going off into the unmarked world. I found a junkyard with old televisions and cars from the 1960s. There was a chimney with no building around it, nothing else, but a chimney. There was old medicine and canning jars in the muddy dirt. I would dig with my little hands and find old jars, take them home and clean them off. My mother liked them. There was an old abandoned cabin, with a torn-up mattress and an old chimney made of stones. I liked spending a lot of time there.

My favorite place was the hardest to find. My brothers showed it to me when I was about six years old and I always remembered exactly where it was. No one ever went there because it was so hard to get to, the only way to get there was to walk by The Monsters, these tall hills where people would drive dirt bikes and four wheelers. Walk past that, down the hill, then you get to Squaw Creek; an old creek, a real creek. I've looked at the maps from 1856, and the creek was there even then. It wasn't manmade at all. I would take a right at the creek, and after that, it was nothing but brambles and prickly bushes. You had to go in knowing you would get cut, that you were going to suffer. I would go alone, no one wanted to do that with me. I would have to crawl and get muddy, getting one cut after another. But after twenty minutes of crawling and bleeding, I would end up at an old dam. It was a small dam, but yes it was a dam. There were two giant blocks of cement, and random blocks scattered under the creek water. I would sit on the cement block looking down at the water. I felt so safe, no one could hurt me there. There were no sounds, only the humming of bugs and squirrels chirping up in the trees.

Sometimes a perch would appear in the water and I would look at it swimming around doing its fish thing.

Ohio was gone though. I didn't know how to eat Dairy Queen anymore.

In South Korea there was forest, but I hardly ever walked in it. I walked the streets. I walked those streets endlessly. Towards the end, I would sit in a bar where no white men went. It was on a street near my house, not in Itaewon or Hongdea but somewhere deep in old Seongnam, a suburb of Seoul. There was a mountain called Namhansanseong, which means the palace south of the Han River. When I would leave my apartment, I would enter the streets of Korea, tall buildings covered with signs and lights, an endless number of glowing signs. I would look to the left, and there was Namhansanseong. In the winter when the leaves had fallen, you could see the walls of the fortress. Several times I walked up the mountain, saw the fortress, saw the palace, and walked into the old Buddhist temples. I bowed to many Buddhas on Namhansanseong. But there were no Buddhas in America, the Grand Canyon had no Buddhas, no temples, no fortresses. Maybe someday society will collapse and there will be strange desert people, and they make fortresses on the cliffs of the Grand Canyon, but it hasn't happened, not yet.

4.

The bus dropped us off at the human resources office, it was all wooden and Western-looking. I smiled just looking at it. I was a little worried that the computer would remember I was there a decade before, and they would tell me I was a dirty drunk and I had to leave, but my records had been deleted and no one remembered me. They made me go to several different rooms and get explanations about how things worked at the park. In one room I sat with an old white man who had been living at the canyon for three years. He was retired and took a job helping with rooms. He told his life story, he had been a good man, he married, had three kids, worked hard as a high school math teacher. He paid his bills, he didn't drink himself to sleep, but he wasn't stuck in his ways, he told us not only did he love the canyon, but if we respected and cared for it, the canyon would love us too.

They sent me to an older woman who would help me get a room. She asked, "Do you want to live in Victor Hall?" I knew the destiny of everyone who lives in Victor Hall, going home and telling everyone you screwed up. I responded firmly, "Can I please not live in Victor Hall?" She laughed and said, "Yes, Victor Annex behind it is a lot quieter, and there's a nice young man that lives there who is very polite."

She handed me the keys, I smiled.

Victor Annex was a building behind Victor Hall and between the cabins. I went into my room, my roommate wasn't there, his bed was perfectly made. There was an old Acer computer. Didn't look cool.

There were blankets and a pillow on the bed folded up, I made the bed, put some of my things in the closet and dresser, looked around the room, realizing it was going to be my home for the next few months.

I felt anxious, I hadn't seen the canyon yet, I wanted to experience it, I left my dorm room and walked toward the canyon. I had to walk over the railroad tracks, a train came from Prescott, mostly German and Japanese tourists rode on it. Halfway between Prescott and the Grand Canyon the train would get robbed by cowboys, the tourists went crazy for it.

On the train tracks I saw three elk and several mule deer. There they were, the animals that lived there. The elk and deer walked peacefully in the park, no one was allowed to shoot them. I stood for a while, looking at them, smiling. The elk were so big and strong. What an animal. An animal that could kill me, but I had no desire to provoke that response.

I went up the black stairs that led up the hill to the Bright Angel Lodge and restaurants. I was getting closer and closer to the canyon. It had been seven years since I had last seen it. What would it look like today? What answers did it have for me?

There it was, the canyon.

I stood there smiling. There was nothing else I could do.

Hermit's Rest

I woke up early and went to the Maswik cafeteria for breakfast. I got a breakfast burrito and a large cup of hot coffee. I hurried and ate my food and got on the bus to Hermit's Rest. My plan was simple, I would take the bus seven miles out to Hermit's Rest and hike all the way back.

The bus was full of tourists from all over the world. There were French, British, Koreans, Australians, Texans from San Antonio, Mormons from Provo, Utah, and there were even Saudi Arabians, all to see the canyon. We all knew why we were there, we didn't have to worry anymore. We were at the rim of the Grand Canyon. As far as we could tell, we had done everything right in life, we must have not made one mistake. We'd saved up our money, we'd counted our pennies, we'd put things on credit cards that we shouldn't have, and we'd taken long uncomfortable plane rides, but we got there, we got to the rim of the Grand Canyon.

When the bus got to Hermit's Rest, I walked around the old stone building. I went inside and saw the giant fireplace in the souvenir shop. I didn't feel like buying anything. I looked, then walked out to look at the canyon. Everyone got back on the bus but I started walking.

My first destination was Pima Point, but who knew how long it would take me to get there.

As I walked the sun got higher and higher, more light came down on me. I was so alone there, it felt like the wind would take me away. Sometimes I would walk on the cement, sometimes I would walk off the path. I didn't see anyone for a long time, I took my shirt off and laid down on a rock. I closed my eyes and went to sleep for a while. When I woke up twenty minutes had passed. I did some yoga on a rock, I let the sun hit me. I wanted the sunlight to penetrate me, to erase those three years in South Korea. I asked the canyon to heal me.

"This is the beginning, this is between me and you, canyon. Can you heal me? I've got some real deep wounds, canyon. You know why I left South Korea, you know what happened there? I can't forget what happened, the scenario plays over and over again. Is there something in you that can make it stop? There is some part of me that believes tomorrow I'll wake up and it'll be over. But the scenario plays over and over again in my mind, and it is becoming one with me. If I can't make it stop soon, it will unify with me and I'll be sad as long as I live. I've come for you to heal me."

Hopi Point Sunset

The guy across the hall from me was named Dream, a wacky name I know, but that was his name. He told me his first name was Ulysses, but he preferred to be called Dream. He was only 22 years old, a big Jamaican man, over six feet tall, with strong beautiful arms.

I was only there for a few days and hadn't made friends yet, but I had talked to Dream a couple of times and he seemed nice. I knocked on Dream's door, he opened it rubbing his eyes, he had been watching a movie on his computer. There was no internet access, everyone had to get DVDs from the recreation center.

"What are you doing?" I said.

"Watching X-Men, I'm worried about calling my mom, my phone isn't working. My phone never works here. My mom is going to be worried, my mom worries about me a lot," said Dream.

I stood there smiling. I said, "I'm sure she'll be fine. Let's go see the sunset at Hopi Point. We need to get on the bus."

"I've never seen a sunset at Hopi Point, can two guys see a sunset together."

"I don't know, I'm lonely, let's go."

Dream told me he was from Montego Bay, studying to run a restaurant or hotel, and he was working as a cook at the El Tovar for the summer. Being at the Grand Canyon was part of a study abroad internship. His parents both worked at hotels and were managers, and his mother made him speak standard American English. I had heard other Jamaicans speak in the dorm, and I could only understand about 70% of what they were saying, but I could understand everything Dream said.

On the bus we started talking about our families, normal "do you have any siblings" talk.

Dream told me, "I had an older brother, but he's dead now. He got into gangs, thought he was cool, wanted to be tough. So he started running around with real crazy people, and he got himself into trouble." Dream paused, then said, "They cut him up, with a machete. They cut him into pieces. Like into pieces, they cut my brother into pieces."

I didn't know what to do say, I tried my best and said, "Like into pieces?"

"Yeah, into pieces. After that my mother, she got real protective of me. I was little then, was about six years younger than my brother. My mother got real protective of me, she never liked when I boasted or tried to look tough. She didn't want me to be tough, she wanted me to be smart. She hardly ever let me out of her sight. It was tough, but I understand, she didn't want me to get into trouble like my older brother." Dream was strangely calm when he said this, he didn't burst into emotion, he just told me. He told me like he had told a million people, and I was one of the next million he had to tell.

I was going to have to tell the truth, but I didn't want to. I didn't want to say. What I was going to say next I had not mentioned in two years. The last time was in a bar in Seoul, I told a stranger, she was pretty and wanted to know. Now I would tell Dream. I never told Americans my real problems, my real pain. It would feel too real to tell an American. I didn't want to say it, but I did anyway, "My brother died too. He was a real big guy, like you. He was six foot four, with broad shoulders. He carried two buck knives, and a shotgun. He became a truck driver, and somehow ended up driving drugs across the border to Mexico. He liked that life, he liked transporting drugs and being around fucked-up people. I've never liked being around fucked-up drug addicts. Drug addicts past the age of 25 are totally creepy to me."

Dream laughed, "I know, older people can smoke weed, but like other drugs, it is weird to me."

"Yeah, but I guess my brother was weird. He did something and pissed someone off, drug addicts are sensitive."

We laughed.

I continued, "Well, he pissed somebody off, and somebody shot him. We got a call from Texas one day that they found my brother shot dead in his truck in Texas. It was about four years ago."

We both sat there, we didn't know what it meant, what had we done wrong to have such a fate? Two dead brothers, two brothers that wouldn't behave.

We got to Hopi Point, there were about a hundred tourists there watching the sunset.

When the sun finally disappeared behind the curvature of the earth, the sky was purple with gold wiggling lines going through it.

The Employee Cafeteria

The employee cafeteria had not changed since I was there in 2000. The same tables, the same pictures on the walls. The only new thing was a flat screen television. The employee cafeteria was located in the Bright Angel building. The Bright Angel had a steakhouse, a bar/coffee shop, a Denny's style restaurant, an ice cream shack, a hotel desk and a souvenir shop. None of it had changed, there were laws against change at the canyon written by the Federal government. The Bright Angel restaurants were meant to remain forever. If people came to the Grand Canyon in 2063 or 2458 The Bright Angel was going to be the same. The Steak House dining room was the only room with permission to change, the rest remained in stasis.

A long hallway connected all the restaurants. Old doors lined the corridor, all of them still with skeleton keys. The Grand Canyon messes with your sense of time. The canyon never changes, the buildings never change, the tourists have always been happy and stressed and worried and moving on to the next place. There were new tourists every day, but they all had the same emotions, exhilaration at seeing the canyon and worry that their kids might fall over the edge.

I worked as a cashier most days in the employee dining room. Workers would come in and stand in line ordering their food. A cook named Pete would make their orders. Pete was an Irish-looking guy from Oklahoma, but he hadn't been back there in years. He could never go home, he said there was always drama, nothing to go home to. He had bounced around the Southwest working in LA, Phoenix, eventually became homeless, someone told him that The Grand Canyon hires anyone, he took a bus up to the canyon and had been there ever since.

An old Navajo woman named Sheila worked the dining room. It was her job to wipe the tables, put away dishes, take out the garbage. She spent most of her time folding napkins. She was 72 years old. One of the first times I talked to her, I said, "I'm from Ohio." She told me she when she was little, she used to live in Steamboat, deep in the Navajo Rez, in a town of less than 300. A bus used to come and pick up the girls and drive them to Cleveland to go to school. I thought for a second she was going to say it was horrible, but no, she said it was beautiful. She loved the trees, she loved Lake Erie, she loved the autumn. She loved Ohio. I didn't mention I hated Ohio, but she hadn't been to Ohio in over 50 years. Maybe if I didn't see Ohio for 50 years I would remember it as a wonderful place.

Sheila laughed all day folding the napkins. She lived with her sister in a little dorm room in Colter Hall built in 1937. Older Navajos from all over the park came and visited her, they would get food and talk with her for the duration of their lunches and head back out to their jobs. She was tough though, she could get angry if you were slacking. If you made her mad she would tell you to your face that what you were doing was stupid.

Sheila had this tattoo on her hand, it said her name "Sheila" right on the back of her hand. I asked her when she got it, she said she and her sister took a cactus needle and did it when they were teenage girls back in Steamboat. She was embarrassed of it, she had lived her life with her own name tattooed on her hand.

After weeks of being in the employee cafeteria, something weird happened. Something my mind always drifts back to, it was so potent I cannot forget it. Two young women walked in, I had never seen them before. They were obviously Eastern European and looked confused. They had never been in America before and were still shaky about the customs. I had just been in Korea, I had been in several countries. I knew the feeling of trying to adjust yourself, of trying to get the world aligned.

Both of the young women wore dresses, they looked at the food and Pete. Pete didn't look at them, Pete never looked at women, he had some kind of emotional blockage when it came to human intimacy, he would die with it, somewhere in America, unnoticed by anyone except a nurse named Carmina from the Philippines who didn't have a loving husband, but did have two kids that were okay.

One of the young women glowed to me. I had emotions, she was giving me emotions. She seemed strangely magical to me. I had not had feelings concerning a woman for a long time, I had forgotten what emotions even felt like. I had a blockage like Pete. I hate to think I had anything in common with Pete, but I did, I had a blockage. I would look around the world at women and feel nothing. It wasn't even forced. I never woke up saying to myself, "Billy, today you will feel nothing about women, you will have no sexual thoughts, you will not get a crush on anyone you meet. If a woman is flirting with you, you will smile and not even notice, that part of your heart that gets crushes and loves is dead." No, I can't say I intentionally did that.

When I looked at the woman standing in line, I felt something.

She and her friend ordered food and came to the register. I sat at the register maintaining a small polite smile, even though I felt overwhelmed by emotions. I showed no appreciation for her, I simply said, "Where are you two from?" They responded somewhere in Poland, not Warsaw, somewhere else, with a cooler name. They didn't ask me anything, they took their burritos and sat down. I looked at them across the room, like a creepy weird older man, being creepy, doing creepy things, living an awesome creepy life at the Grand Canyon.

They looked at their burritos and laughed, they spoke Polish to each other. I didn't understand what they were saying, I assumed it was funny comments concerning burritos.

Javelinas

I had a mission. I was going to walk into the forested part between the railroad and the West Rim road. It was probably not a good idea, no one ever did it, no one ever left the trails. But there was a part of me that didn't care if I died. During those days, I felt like life was endless. All I could see was endless life ahead of me. There were no locations, no stopping points, there were no candles in any windows. The world had no place for me, I wasn't even being sad, I wasn't even having self-pity, I had no interest in anyone telling me, "It is going to get better." The banal platitudes of my country would not save me. All my friends were in Korea, or they had gone back to their homes in America, but I had no home. Wherever I was, I was just there, and that's all.

On the way out the door, Dream was walking down the hall and asked me where I was going, I said to the forested part. He told me, "Man, I am scared to go there. Are you allowed to go there?"

"Hmm, I don't think anyone will care. Do you want to come?"

He stood there thinking about it and said, "Yeah, let me get the right shoes on."

Dream and I walked down the railroad tracks. Dream said, "I don't know if my mom wants me going in here, she says there are rattlesnakes. I might run if I see a rattlesnake."

"If there are rattlesnakes it will be okay. They won't even notice us."

"I don't understand how a rattlesnake couldn't notice us," said Dream.

"Because they are busy. When we are afraid of snakes, we are projecting ourselves onto the snakes. We are making the snakes aware

31

of us, but really they are snakes, and they are doing their snake thing They have places to go and things to do, they know what they are doing, they aren't looking for humans to bite."

That calmed him a bit.

Right before we entered the forested part, I said, "We have to walk quietly if we are going to see something. Walk like this." I picked my foot up and then put it down on my toes softly, and then mindfully pushed the back of my foot down. "See how quiet that is? You try."

Dream, even though he was a big man, did the same kind of steps.

"Okay, let's be quiet," I said.

We slowly walked through the forested part. There were old Utah Junipers everywhere, little tiny cactus balls on the ground. I stepped on a cactus ball, I felt the spikes drive into my foot. I wanted to be angry but I didn't care. I let it happen. Dream was like, "Oh shit, Billy, you stepped on a cactus." I was like, "Yes."

We sat down on the ground. I took my shoe off and picked the needles out. The bottom of my foot was bleeding a little but it wasn't bad.

We stood up and walked. I realized we were lost but I didn't tell Dream, he seemed to have full trust in me. It felt good that anyone trusted me.

As we were walking we heard noises, we both stopped. I loved hearing noises in the woods, I loved feeling the rush that something big and scary might be hiding behind a tree, ready to eat me. The desire to be eaten was overwhelming at times, but I didn't tell anyone. Dream and I walked toward the noise. I looked back and

Dream looked nervous, like he wanted to go back but he had to live up to a certain level of masculinity and keep going.

And there they were, a small family of javelinas, little pig like creatures covered in fur. There was a mom and three kids about 30 yards away. I pointed at them and Dream looked, his face lit up, our faces were full of excitement. The mom looked at us, then suddenly dashed ahead five yards toward us, stopped and made a noise. We both got scared, neither of us had javelina training. We both picked trees and got up in them. We were both only four feet above the ground, but that was enough. Javelinas can't climb trees.

The mother javelina realized we were no threat. We weren't going to come any closer to her babies. We stood on branches in the trees, looking at the family living their lives. They were just living outside among the rain and cold and heat.

To the Bottom of the Canyon:
Down Kaibab up Bright Angel Trail

On the bus heading down the west rim, six in the morning, looking out the window. Barely anyone on the bus. I decided I would hike down to the bottom of the canyon. I hadn't done it in over a decade and knew I had to do it again. The shimmering green world had always haunted me. I had to get back. The Grand Canyon had something to say to me, some truth, I knew it was down there, I just needed to get to the bottom.

The bus stopped at Yaki Point, the sun barely up, a pale light. I went over to the water bottle filling station and loaded up six bottles, put them in my backpack. The bag was heavy on my back, but I knew I had to carry it. There was no water on Kaibab Trail. There wasn't going to be any water until I got to Bright Angel Trail.

I started hiking down, there were tourists at the beginning, all bumbling around holding one bottle of water. I walked by them telling everyone good morning, hello, have a nice day. I smiled and felt good.

I had not smiled in a long time, happiness was not there for me, I couldn't find it anywhere. I used to have a shit-eating grin. I used to smile, I used to feel enthusiasm, things changed, I felt no enthusiasm anymore. I would hear my favorite songs, and they sounded like dead noise. My favorite movies would come on and I would fall asleep before the exposition was over. I would encounter beautiful women, women I usually found entertaining, women that captivated me, and I wouldn't even notice. A month earlier, I was sitting next to a woman at a bar, after three hours she said, "Billy, I'm trying to sleep with you, don't you care." I responded, "Oh, I never noticed."

I was smiling though, as I entered the canyon. I stumbled down through the cliff faces and white colored rocks. Eventually the tourists holding one water bottle disappeared, now there were tourists with backpacks with three water bottles heading to Cedar Ridge. As each moment passed, it got hotter and hotter. Everyone told me, "It is hot down at the bottom." I believed them. I took my shirt off and let the sun hit me.

When I got to Cedar Ridge there were some families there, a restroom and posts to tie mules to. There were no mules, only families. I hung out for twenty minutes, drank some water. I started to sweat, I could feel that hiking feeling come over me, my toes were hurting from being pounded into the front of my shoes from walking downhill. Cedar Ridge had no shade, I had to rest in the open sun.

The deeper you go into the Grand Canyon, the more desert it becomes. Little cactuses, jack rabbits and lizards. I came upon a train of mules carrying goods up from the bottom. Wranglers, strong men and women rode the mules.

After the mule train was over, I hiked on, kept moving down Kaibab Trail. There was a rich man and his son, the rich guy bought several thousand dollars in gear to walk down the trail. His backpack was huge, something designed for a two-week trip to Alaska. He and his son had on REI clothes, Merrell shoes, everything brand new, they were totally set, the dad didn't know what he was doing, he had gone to school to be a lawyer or doctor, or maybe he owned a business and had too much money. He was used to buying expensive things, that was his identity, and he maintained it even at the bottom of the canyon. I didn't laugh at them, I asked them how they were doing, the dad looked tired. The dad was with his son, I could see my childhood for a second, there it was in my mind, a vision. That engulfed me, tangled me all up. I was in Sigel, Pennsylvania, on the old dirt road leading up to Grandpa's cabin. A stone and wood cabin built on 500 acres of land deep in the forest, it was decorated with deer antlers, at least 30 antlers with the names of the hunters that brought them down and the years written on the wood. There were rattlesnake skins, a strange voodoo head one of my grandpa's friends brought back from his time in the military, a tank bullet from World War II and a strange picture of a marlin in the sea so covered in dust it gave the painting a texture of its own.

When I was seven years old my grandpa and his friends fascinated me. They had all been in World War II. One man had been at the Battle of the Bulge, another in the South Pacific, another escaped the violence by being a cook. They and their wives had lived through the Great Depression, the war. They were real men, they drank beer, ate meat and killed animals. Their arms and chests were strong, but they were also members of the Masons, the Kiwanis, and local historical societies. They participated in local politics and gave to charity. When I was little they were kind to me, and there in the canyon I realized they were dead. The men of my childhood had died. I started to worry that I had no cabin for children, that I had no antlers with my name on them, and I never would.

The vision ended with me waking up in the old cabin as a child on a cold fall morning, going down and sitting at the big wooden table where we played cards the night before. I was smiling, it was true and I felt safe. I looked at my grandpa, a big man, a man that killed rattlesnakes, a man that once carried a deer two miles on his back after killing it with a single shot and gutting it with a buck knife. He had fought in the war, then became a trucker, he'd had four kids and they were all fed. He wasn't perfect, a bit of a cheater and he drank too much Black Velvet, but I didn't know that then. He was this big man, a man much bigger and more determined than my father. I always felt safe around my grandpa, I knew he would protect me. Grandpa would make me hot chocolate, scrambled eggs and sausage all while calling me his "right-hand man." That's what he would tell people when I was with him, "Here's Billy, he's my right-hand man." He died while I was in Korea.

After the vision was over, I wasn't smiling. There I was alone, on Kaibab Trail. I was no one's right-hand man alone on that trail.

Farther down the canyon I went, my body started to hurt. I was getting a case of "the wants." I wanted to get to the river, I wanted to see the river, thinking if I could get to the river, it would mean something. I had to tell myself, the river has no answer, each step is the answer, you're in the canyon, you're okay, don't bother yourself having to get somewhere.

Before getting to the river, you go through a tunnel carved out of the rock. I wanted that river, I walked through the tunnel and came out on a metal bridge. A great feeling came over me. I had made it to the bottom of the Grand Canyon. No one would ever be able to take that from me, and that's what I needed badly, one thing no one could take away from me. Experiences are the best things to get, because they can't be taken away.

My mind stupidly thought, "I wish she could see me here. I want her to feel proud of me." A ghost had chased me to the bottom of the canyon. I didn't like myself for thinking that, I wished I would stop thinking thoughts like that, but I guess that was not the day I was going to stop thinking those thoughts.

For an hour I hiked along the river toward Bright Angel Trail, I stopped at picnic tables and ate lunch. There was a strong creek there with water from the river, I laid in it to cool myself down. For a minute I wanted the water to wash me away, to carry me down the Colorado. I would end up in the Pacific Ocean, a shark would eat me.

I worked my way out of the canyon, up Bright Angel trail. As I was walking I saw a bighorn sheep. He jumped out in front of me, I was alone, the bighorn sheep looked right at me, and said, "Hello, I'm Solon."

I smiled and replied, "If you are Solon, who are the happiest men that ever lived?"

Solon grinned and said, "There were two very happy men, one was named Marcus Tullius Cicero. He served his people with sincerity, generosity and energy. He believed in the beauty of each citizen, and how each citizen could contribute and make a strong commonwealth. He had a wife and children, he worked in society, he was a moral man. When the soldiers came to execute him, he didn't complain, he didn't plead for his life, he didn't scorn the government for killing him even though he spent his whole life trying to make that government better. He lifted his chin and let his neck be split open."

"Who was the other man?"

"The other was Dazu Huike, the Second Patriarch of Zen. This man was very different than Cicero, Dazu Huike was alone in the world. He had no wife, no children, he had no money and never had any power. He spent his life seeking and perfecting his enlightenment. And spent his later years spreading the dharma, not waging wars and getting into controversies. Still, the government could not stand a man like Dazu Huike, they considered him a freak of nature, a creature so incomprehensible that he had to be killed. And just like Cicero, they cut his head off. Both of these men were decapitated, both of them died fearlessly. They knew how to live and how to die, one for society and one for enlightenment."

I smiled and hiked on, the bighorn sheep leaped into the brush and I never saw him again.

Exhaustion had arrived. I could feel myself wanting to stop. I was alone, walking and walking, putting one foot in front of the other, my mind started to fizzle out. Coherent thoughts about my life didn't come anymore. Finally I was getting to my goal of complete mental breakdown. That's why I came to the canyon, to destroy my mind. For months it had given me nothing but agony. But there I was walking through Indian Gardens with no thoughts, no thoughts of the past, no thoughts of the present and no thoughts of the future. A breeze would hit me and that was all. I would pass a cool rock formation, I would touch it with my hands, put my cheek on the rocks, close my eyes, and that was all, nothing but the feeling of the rock on my face.

After moving my feet for hours, I finally made it to a faucet that shot out cold water, I put my whole body under the faucet, letting the water soak it. I had no sense of embarrassment, I knew I didn't look good, in no other situation would I allow myself to be completely soaked by water. But there I was, pummeling my body with cold water. I needed it, I needed the cold water to shock me awake, to give me power to keep hiking, to keep me moving my feet.

After Indian Gardens I was heading up the canyon switchbacks, one switchback after another, where was I going? Who was I on those switchbacks? I wasn't me, I wasn't Billy Cox. The canyon had no intention of naming me, the canyon didn't care about my childhood, the canyon didn't care about what happened in Korea, the canyon didn't care if I died there or made it to the top. The canyon preferred nothing.

I hiked by a couple in their upper thirties, they were white, slightly overweight and Northwestern. They were covered with sweat, their whole bodies looked strained. I asked them how long they had been hiking, they said nine hours. But they had started from the bottom, they were taking a break at the end of every switchback. The woman said she was from Seattle and had always dreamed of hiking to the bottom of the Grand Canyon. She had made it, but she was paying the price for having a wild dream like that. Somewhere else on the planet there was a married couple in the Caribbean at that moment, drunk on a beach, lying in the sand, and then there were those two, sweating and begging God for mercy at every switchback.

I knew I had to keep going, I needed to get to the top by nine, the cafeteria would close at ten and I would be screwed for food. To me there was no point in stopping. If my legs could move, let them move. I did a sun salutation and kept moving my feet, one after another.

I began to feel the ground beneath my feet, step by step, step step step, pick up your legs Billy, pick up those feet. Started to have visions of football in the humid Ohio summer, middle-aged men yelling at young boys to run faster, to hit harder, to not be lazy. They were always screaming about us being lazy and not giving 110%. I always gave 110%, I always hit the hardest, I always tried to finish laps in the first five, I always wanted to win. There I was, on a switchback on Bright Angel Trail, 2000 miles from Ohio, 10,000 miles from Korea, and still yelling at myself in the voice of those football coaches. Everyone put pressure on me, as soon as the teachers realized I could get A's, they turned the screws, kindergarten through 12th. As soon as the coaches realized I was fast and could hit, they were turning the screws on Billy Cox.

And then in college, all over again, professors, fellow students, girlfriend, everyone turning the screws on Billy Cox. Everywhere, on TV, on billboards, on the sides of buses, everyone turning the screws on Billy Cox, screaming at me to do better, because I was better, I was stronger, I was smarter. Everyone expected great things from me, but I couldn't deliver. Visions of my grandpa's death again, when he died they listed all of his descendants and their spouses, everyone was married and had kids but me. My name was alone, the only name alone, I was the only one with a master's, the only one that had lived abroad, the only one that read *Infinite Jest* all the way through, but I was alone.

Grandpa's right-hand man was alone on a switchback in the Grand Canyon. I sat on a log and drank water. I rubbed my eyes, visions of Grandpa, is this what he really wanted for me? His idea of nature was the forest of Pennsylvania, sitting in a tree-stand for hours wearing camouflage, waiting for a buck to come along. Standing by a clear creek trying to catch trout, holding his caught trout in his hand, showing it to his friends, making jokes about the size of fish the other guys caught. That was his nature, that wasn't mine. My obsession with nature had grown and grown until I found myself tired, sweaty, with sore knees and feet on a switchback on Bright Angel Trail.

Even though, at that moment, I was doing something incredibly hard, something most people would never do, I had never felt so weak. A real weakness came over me. I couldn't stop thinking, "Grandpa's right-hand man, Grandpa's right-hand man, Grandpa's right-hand man." I asked my mother once if he said that about his other grandkids, she replied, "No, only you. He told me once there was something special about you, something unbreakable, but at the same time he said you had no sense, that he had never met anyone with so little common sense in his life, and that he felt sad for you because he knew your life would be strangely hard, he knew this because he had met a few men like you in his life, when he was younger he was scared of them, but he knew in his old age, that there were men out there who lived different lives, and you were going to be one of them."

The top of the canyon would not come, I kept walking and walking. The visions ended, I truly couldn't think any longer, my consciousness was wiped out. I felt as if at any moment I could have laid down and gone to sleep, but I also felt that I could make it, that there was an end to Bright Angel Trail.

I was on my last switchback, almost done, and there were two Koreans. I could hear the Korean words being spoken, it felt like a joke, I had hiked 17 miles to destroy my past and in the last 50 yards I returned to Korea. I told them hello, we talked about Seoul for a little bit, then I finished the hike.

When I got to the top, I sat on the cement walkway. Tourists taking pictures looked at me, they asked if I'd done it, I said yes, I had done it. They were happy, they would never do it, but they liked the idea of someone doing it. A little boy was there from Northern Africa, Algeria or Egypt, I don't know. He looked at my sweaty body, my face strained and ugly. His dad told him what I did, and the boy smiled.

Christian Ministry Services

I was not a Christian, nor did I have any interest in becoming one. My parents had raised me without religion. There was an old bible in a closet, but that was about it. In my twenties I got interested and read several books from the Old Testament and the Gospels, but not really to get closer to God. When I was getting my English degree I had to read a lot of novels by dead people who referenced religious things. I felt that maybe I was missing something, that it was hindering my understanding of the novels, so I read through the Bible, Koran, histories on their religions and a history of the Jewish people. But never had I felt "religious." I never felt a chill run through me, never lost myself in song to the otherworldly gods.

I have often wondered, have I believed in anything? Have I ever cared about anything so much I would have died for it? The answer was probably no. In Korea I met a woman in her forties, from Ireland. Her husband was working at the base in Seoul and she was teaching English at a local high school. She told me, "You never fully give yourself. You act vulnerable, you confess a lot, but you refuse to let the last inch go. You refuse to compromise. Love is compromise, Billy. I met my husband in Italy, I had a good job in Italy, I had a life there, I had friends. Fuck, I was in Italy, who doesn't want to live in Italy? But I left, the man I loved asked me to leave, and I did. And after he finishes up in Seoul, we are going to America to live. I'm doing it, I'm compromising."

As I was sitting on the dead carcass of a Utah Juniper outside the dorms, I remembered that when I was in the cafeteria earlier in the day, a guy named Nate, an American from Portland, told me he was leading Christian Services on the edge of the canyon at twilight. Nate was friendly, he had short hair, a skinny body and was always articulate, but never obnoxious or in your face about his religion. He hiked from the South Rim to the North Rim and back in three days. He would jog the first mile and a half of Bright Angel down and then back up. He loved being in motion, he loved movement and action, being part of things. Nothing about him reminded me of those traditional Christians screaming on the television. He always hung out with Chandra, a cute young woman with blonde hair from Texas, who said hi to everyone and never forgot anyone's name, where they were from, how many kids they had. It was like her mind was a database of everyone's life. She had a funny story though, she was half Jewish and had all these cool Hebrew tattoos on her back. She said it was because she didn't want to forget who she was, even if she was Christian, half of her was the entire history of the Jewish people.

I stood up from the dead tree and began to walk toward the edge of the canyon where the Christian services were being held. I felt no fear doing this, I was just a guy walking past mule deer and elk on the way to the edge of the canyon. The animals were there and I was there, we were both occupying a space close together, within visual distance of each other.

At the edge of the canyon around ten people were sitting, I recognized most of them from the employee cafeteria. Nate and Chandra were there, they both waved at me. We were truly on the edge of the canyon. There weren't chairs, there weren't walls. The edge, the cliff was right there, we all could have jumped off if we wanted to at any moment. But we didn't, we stayed on the edge, sitting peacefully.

I found a flat rock, folded my legs up and sat down with a little smile. Not a shit-eating grin. I wasn't acting, like I usually did, but actually smiling a little.

A young man from Kentucky came out and gave a speech on the ministry of the National Parks. This speech was read before every service, it was part of Federal Law that the National Park Services couldn't endorse any religion. The young man stated that it was a program run between the church community and the park services, that the services were provided by college students from all over America. That the service would be non-denominational, that any Christian could participate in the services, it didn't matter if they were Baptist, Methodist or Catholic.

After the speech was given, Nate walked over with a guitar. He and Chandra began to play hymns. We were all given song books. Nate would direct us to a page and we would sing along. I still didn't lose myself though, I was singing, but I remained neurotic and nihilistic the entire time. The nihilism wouldn't end at that church service. When would the nihilism end? I would always ask myself, when would I wake up and feel something strong enough to make me commit to anything in life? It happened around me all the time, but never for me, I always felt like I was pushing my own body up a cliff like Sisyphus. That's probably how most people felt, or maybe they resigned themselves to the Great Whatever of Life.

Nate put down his guitar and everyone singing sat down. Nate was by himself in front of the great Grand Canyon, a 277-mile-long canyon formed over five million years by the rushing of the Colorado River, Nate stood before one of God's great creations giving a speech on the glory of God. Nate didn't talk about homosexuals or transgender people. He picked a verse out and talked about his feelings on that verse.

While Nate talked I couldn't keep my mind focused. Never having attended church except for weddings and funerals, thinking about Jesus was difficult for me. My mind had three competing versions of Jesus taken from movies and hearsay. The first version was a George Carlin Jesus that was stupid and trite, there were these bureaucrats called Priests that did horrible things like molest children and start wars. The next version was Elmer Gantry Jesus, the TV pastor asking for money, a money Jesus. You give money to God and God rewards you in the here and now with gifts. The third was suffering Catholic Jesus. This bloody figure in human history, this man who lived out in the wilderness of ancient Palestine. What a world that had to be, my mind said, a world with nothing but stone huts and animals. A world without newspapers, medicine, statistical evidence or scientific research. A world without due process and self-incrimination laws. I always liked that Jesus was arrested, that he was a loser, a big loser in his world. Jesus went on trial and they convicted him, they concluded he was guilty. No other religion had the audacity to make their God such a loser. The Buddhists made their prophet a prince, the Muslims made Muhammad a merchant and a general, the Prophets of the Jewish texts were all wealthy landowners or royalty. But Jesus was a loser.

Nate didn't talk about how Jesus was a loser, he talked about how we can find the Bible anywhere if we look, that the Bible made life coherent and reasonable if we let it.

Nate picked up the guitar and sang more songs. The sun began to set on the service. There I was, on the edge of the Grand Canyon, hearing a real service. It felt worth it, I would have never gone to a service in a church, but there on the edge of the canyon, in the open air, religion felt right. The kind of religion I had always wanted, an open-air religion.

After the service was over, everyone stood up slowly and smiled. I didn't tell anyone about my Jesus was a loser idea. It was just a dumb passing thought, a needless stream of mental events that didn't need to be shared.

We all talked for a little bit, then I walked back to my dorm alone. There were elk by the train track, tourists from Japan and France were taking pictures of them. I stood for a little bit looking.

Victor Hall

It was early in the night. I bought a six pack of beer and walked over to Victor Hall, there were some people hanging out, drinking beer and doing nothing. I sat on the old stone porch and waited for the weirdos to arrive. The first weirdos were two guys named Scott and Jeff, they were American and basically homeless. They had ended up at the canyon because of unknown reasons. Everyone assumed Scott was a drug dealer. He was a big white guy from Utah, probably Mormon, currently an ex-Mormon, but one day he would clean up and be Mormon again. Scott lived with an attractive Filipino girl who never spoke, she did her make-up and drugs. Jeff was from California, no one knew why he was at the canyon. He told everyone something different, one story was his brother got him a job there, one story was he was running from the law, and another version was he always dreamed of the canyon, but nothing added up to be a conclusive truth.

Scott walked up the porch with his Filipina girlfriend. He yelled, "What are you guys doing? I'm Russian, I'm a boxer. I have boxed, I'll box everyone on this porch." I didn't look at him, I knew he would leave eventually. He continued, "I was born to box, I'm Russian, Russians are great fighters, I'm a great fighter, just like Russians are great fighters." Then he started picking cigarette butts out of the ashtray. He picked one out and lit it. The girl stood by his side saying nothing, she always looked surprised but not by him, by nothing. I never attempted to speak to her.

Jeff held up a bottle of Absinthe, he yelled, "This is Absinthe, I'm so drunk." I believed him, it was obvious, he was drunk.

Then Money Mike came outside, a little African-American man from Chicago. Money Mike had a million problems. A couple of kids thousands of miles away, child support, an ex-wife, a million problems. Maszov from Poland named him Money Mike, because Maszov gave everyone nicknames. Money sounded good with Mike in his Polish mind, therefore Maszov called him Money Mike.

Money Mike went up to Scott and said, "My last name is Spinks, like Leon Spinks." Money Mike was drunk also. Money Mike continued, "Do you know who Leon Spinks is?"

Scott yelled back, Scott could actually not stop yelling, "Who the fuck is Leon Spinks?"

"Leon Spinks was a boxer, he was a real boxer. Leon Spinks beat Muhammad Ali!!!"

"Is that your dad?" Said Jeff.

"No, Leon Spinks is not my dad, I have the Spinks last name," Money Mike said.

Scott replied, "I'm Russian! I am a real boxer."

Then Money Mike came over to me, "Billy, you got any smokes, I know you smoke those good American Spirits, can I get one?"

I nodded my head and gave him one. Then he said, "Can I get a beer?"

"Do you have two dollars?" I gave him a beer for two dollars.

Then Scott yelled, "I gotta go, I got important things to do. I'm an important man in this park, I own this Grand Canyon." Jeff followed him into the dorm.

Then an old Navajo man came out holding a guitar. He would always say things to people, but no one ever understood what he was saying. He always looked really sincere when talking, like what he was saying seemed really vital, but it never was, because if it was vital things would have gone differently, but things always went the same. When he spoke Navajo to other Navajos, they understood him perfectly.

The old Navajo drank some Budweiser, then sat down and started strumming. No one asked him to play, no one was paying for a performance. But usually once a night he would walk outside after he got pretty drunk and would play for approximately twenty minutes, then disappear.

The old Navajo who no one could understand started strumming the intro to "Big River" by Johnny Cash and then started singing. His voice came out clear and strong. It didn't make any sense, three minutes earlier he was acting insane and we couldn't understand a word he said, but there it was, a beautiful voice singing out into the Grand Canyon night.

After he was done, a middle-aged white man in his forties with scruffy hair wearing a baseball cap said, "I loved a woman down in Phoenix, but she doesn't want me anymore."

The old Navajo looked at him, shook his head, then said something no one understood. Then he hit the notes for "Wide Open Road," he sang while smiling, even though it was a very sad song. I looked at him singing smiling too, everyone was smiling. He even played the solo. When he finished, the old Navajo said something to the white man in the baseball hat. I didn't understand what he said, but I knew he told the white man, "I sleep alone too, and I got a woman in Kayenta who loves a man that ain't me." If the women in question were here to see these two men right now, they would probably roll their eyes.

The old Navajo smiled at everyone, and went back up to his room to fall asleep.

Next came Maszov and Andrew, a big burly Polish guy who believed he was a philosopher and a little white guy that pounded vodka all night. Maszov loved me, he found out I had a master's degree and considered me worth talking to about things he considered worth talking about. He loved to tell me about when it snowed in Warsaw, and how he had walked down the streets of Warsaw with a beautiful woman. He was young, twenty-two, and still felt fascinated by beautiful women. I no longer held that fascination. I remembered being a young man though in my early twenties and being overwhelmed by the body of a woman, how the need to touch a woman surged through me, how I would obsess over asking women out, what to say around women I had crushes on, if I was making a good impression, did I smell good, was she the one. But on that porch, I had none of those anxieties. Women were just people, they were sad, they wanted approval, some had self-awareness, some were narcissists, and some were shallow, just like men. Maszov still had the idea though in his mind that there were "beautiful women" and snow and Warsaw. I had once held a beautiful woman's hand in New York City, in Seoul, and once in Madrid. It was all gone, bones in my hands. Underneath it all, there was nothing but bones.

Andrew was a little American guy who got a job at the canyon because of his brother, his brother was the assistant manager of one of the hotels, didn't drink a lot and had his own room and a Filipina girlfriend. Almost every male manager under forty had a Filipina girlfriend. Andrew's main concerns were sci-fi, not science, he had no interest in getting a degree in a scientific field at an accredited university, he read a lot of sci-fi novels and dreamed of going to outer space to meet aliens, *Star Trek*, more *Star Trek* than *Star Wars*.

Maszov said to me, "Billy, you know what singularity is?"

"When we become robots?"

"Yeah, but like we become one with the robots and the universe! That is the future, a world where we become one with the machines."

"If I was a machine, could I get drunk?"

"No, you would be a happy machine," Maszov said.

"I really like being sad, I'm pretty good at it."

"No, we won't have to work anymore, we will be machines!"

"Who builds the machines?" I said.

"The machines build the machines."

"At like a factory?"

"We don't have to care about those things, we will be enjoying virtual reality," said Maszov.

"How will people get jobs if the jobs are done by machines?"

"Then people will finally have total justice and freedom to enjoy personal activities like music and poetry."

"I already enjoy poetry and music, I don't need robots to help me do that."

Andrew just sat there, not laughing, randomly sipping on his vodka.

Maszov said, "Billy, you have to understand this is the future. The future is computers. Technology is getting better and better, soon we will have total singularity with the machines."

Then a mule deer walked by the porch, everyone stopped. We all looked at the deer. Maszov looked at the deer and really loved it, he smiled big, like a child. He looked at me and said, "Billy, it is a deer."

"Yes," I said.

The deer stayed for a long time, Maszov lost his train of thought and said, "Do you want to meet some girls Billy?"

I hadn't "met girls" in a long time, not since before Korea. It took a long time for my mind to wrap around the idea of "meeting girls." Lately my mind had been more focused on wanting to see a mountain lion or a pink rattlesnake than wanting to meet a girl.

Maszov yelled to come on. I got up and started walking, carrying a six pack with three bottles of beer left in it. We had to walk through the darkness. In the Grand Canyon National Park there are no outdoor lights, no street lights, no bright beams anywhere, just darkness, so there is at least one place where people may still see the stars.

We had to walk over the train track, while we were crossing it Andrew spotted a big elk close by and yelled, "Oh my god, an elk," and ran back a little. I stood for a moment and looked at the big elk, it wasn't bothering anyone. We walked over the track and made it to the cabins where other employees of the park lived. There were also tourist cabins mainly reserved for Contiki tourists from Australia.

When I was at the park in 2000 the cabins never became part of my life, I remember one time going into a cabin and meeting a young woman that read Ayn Rand and not liking her very much.

As we were walking to the cabins Maszov kept telling us how beautiful the girls were. The one Maszov liked was named Kaja and the other girl was named Marcelina. He kept saying they were from Poznan and not Warsaw. They were not as urban and worldly as him. That he went to a big school and they went to a smaller one. I didn't care what school they went to, we were just guys walking through the darkness of the Grand Canyon.

We got to the door of "the girls." At that moment, boredom was my dominating feeling, I was just following Maszov. Why was I following Maszov, what provoked me to follow a strange Polish man around in the night? But my whole life was like that, I always said yes. I wanted action, I believed that if I said yes enough times it would eventually lead to excitement, to thrills. The people I graduated from high school and college with stopped this by age thirty. They had families, had jobs. They wore khakis and polo shirts. Most of my friends from my master's program had already attained jobs at universities or had written books or gotten jobs at high schools. They were all functioning citizens of the republic.

I stood behind Maszov and Andrew. Maszov knocked on the door, the door opened and there was the woman from the cafeteria. Everything changed at that moment, my boredom had left, my enthusiasm regained.

We went into the cabin. It was a small space with two beds and it was a little hot. There was no television or radio, a few books, that was all. Maszov introduced me to the woman that opened the door, she said, "My name is Kaja," and I said, "My name is Billy." Then

Marcelina introduced herself. Kaja was skinny but muscular, she had a big forehead and a cute nose. Her hands were wispy and her legs, well, perfect. Marcelina was also muscular and strong-looking. She was a somewhat shorter than Kaja, both were very cool.

We all sat on beds. I sat on a bed with Maszov, Andrew remained standing holding his vodka bottle, at this point he couldn't even speak. Kaja and Marcelina sat on a bed together.

Maszov immediately started speaking in Polish. Then they all burst into Polish. I didn't mind this at all. When I was in Korea I spent most of my life with people around me speaking Korean, not including me at all. And really that was my life. It was as if most days I was deaf, I learned to be deaf, I learned not to care what people were saying in other languages.

I looked around the room, trying to find anything I could talk about, I saw a plastic jar of peanut butter. I looked Kaja in the eyes with a little smile and said, "Do you like peanut butter?" She looked me back in the eyes, and said, "Yes, I like peanut butter very much."

I said slowly, the same way I spoke to Koreans who were learning English, "Do you make sandwiches or put it on crackers? Do you have any jelly?"

She replied, "We put it on crackers, but most of the time we scoop it out and eat it, we don't even put it on bread."

"What about jelly?"

"We don't have refrigerator, we cannot have cold things."

The more we talked, the bigger our smiles got. Maszov and Marcelina noticed this while they were talking Polish. Andrew noticed nothing, he kept sipping vodka, going deeper into inebriation.

Maszov told Kaja and Marcelina how I had spent three years in South Korea, I could hear a word sounding like Korea being spoken by all of them. After Maszov was done, Kaja said, "You lived in Korea?"

"Yes, I was an English teacher at a university."

"Did you learn Korean?" said Kaja.

"I learned a lot of words, and could say little things, but not too much. I have never been good at learning languages."

She smiled and said, "What is the word for cat?"

I laughed and said, "Goyangi, that is an easy one."

"Hmm, what is crazy?" Then she looked at me like I better know the answer.

I responded, "Michin."

She responded, "Me," then she pointed at her chin and said, "Me-chin?"

"Yes, michin."

Then she says, "Can you write in Korean?"

"Yes, do you want me to write your name?"

"Yes, of course."

I wrote, "가자" and said, "It means, 'Let's go.'"

"Let's go?"

"Yes, let's go. Do you know any other languages besides English?"

"Si, Español. I lived in Spain for nine months going to school. I think I know Spanish better, my English is not good yet."

"Wow, you lived in Spain."

"Yes, in Madrid, I went to the Universidad Complutense de Madrid. It was founded in 1499 by Rodrigo Borgia, Pope Alexander VI. Do you know the Borgia family?"

"Yes, Cesare, Lucrezia and the Saint Francis Borgia, I was born on his Saint day."

She looked impressed, "Wow, an American who knows the Borgias!"

I didn't know what to say or do, I decided to smile and look friendly, because I felt friendly.

We talked for about twenty more minutes, sporadically they would talk in Polish and then come back to English, Marcelina never really bothered with me. At one point she asked me if I liked Katy Perry, I didn't remember at any point in my life having any thoughts about Katy Perry. She was like a famous person who sang music, that was all I knew, but I didn't want to make her sad, I said I liked Katy Perry, she told me that Katy Perry filmed a video in Poland and that she was in it and that she had met Katy Perry, the only time Marcelina looked happy was when she was talking about Katy Perry.

When we were leaving Kaja said to me that they were going to come to the cafeteria tomorrow for lunch, I told her I would be there and we would talk.

As I was walking through the darkness back to the dorm I had emotions, but I didn't know what they meant. How does one even kiss a European? I remembered the first time I ever kissed a Korean woman. The first night we didn't kiss, we had mutual friends and we ended up sleeping on the floor of a friend's apartment after a hard night of partying in Itaewon. It was a freezing winter night and like most guys in Korea he didn't have enough blankets. He threw one blanket at us and we had to share, while we were falling asleep I touched her ribs with my hand, not even her skin, just her sweater. Several days later she texted me, "You touched my ribs."

I remember being on the bus staring at that text, no one had ever said such a pretty thing to me.

A week later we were in Itaewon again. We walked off alone and sat in the Seoul Pub. We were drinking and she looked at me, her eyes never left mine, and we kissed with our mouths open. It hit me that she was somewhere in Korea right at that moment, probably waking up in her tiny apartment, eating breakfast, getting ready for school or work, or whatever she did.

Finding Samantha

I woke up around 2am to go to the bathroom. My roommate was gone, he always slept at his girlfriend's dorm. We never spoke anyway. I don't even remember what his name was, he was twenty-four and had been living at the canyon for several years. He didn't even hike, he didn't own any hiking gear whatsoever. I never heard him mention the canyon, he played games on his computer and read fantasy novels about knights and elves. One time he broke his tooth and couldn't get it fixed because he had no money and the canyon offered no dental care, he didn't care, he lived with a broken tooth. He wasn't there, I woke up alone.

I left my room and headed down to the community bathroom. At night the South Rim was cold, a chilly air would breeze down the hallway through the open doors of the dorm. We hardly ever closed the doors at night, mainly because none of us cared, and we all went to bed drunk or at least tipsy. Sometimes you would be walking down the hallway at night and see a raccoon in the hallway, it wasn't hard to get them away though, throw a couple of things in their direction and they would run out of the building.

I went to the bathroom at the far end, then started back down the long cold hallway to my room. Then I spotted something on the fire escape stairway that led to the second floor. I was like, what is that? That doesn't look normal. I kept walking until I got outside and there was a human on the metal staircase in the open chilly air. It was a woman. I patted her shoulder and said, "Ma'am, are you okay? Wake up, ma'am."

She didn't wake up, was she dead?

I patted her shoulder more, "Ma'am, you have to get up. It is cold outside, are you okay?"

She moved her body a little. I could see her face, it was Samantha, an American woman from the cabins. I didn't know anything about her, I knew she lived with Jessica, the American woman from Connecticut who worked in the ice cream shop with me. I knew that Samantha owned a stick shift Laser and that she liked cheap wine. How does someone fall asleep on a metal staircase in the midst of a chilly wind?

I patted her shoulder more. "Samantha wake up, you gotta go home, I'll help you to the cabins, I'll walk you there."

I went back to my room and put on a pair of cargo shorts, a shirt and my sneakers. When I got back to Samantha she was still sleeping. I looked around and saw no one, there was no one but me awake, no one was there to care about my predicament.

"Samantha, you have to wake up, you can't sleep out here." No response.

"Samantha, come on, you can do this." Samantha stood up, but I could tell there was no hope in getting back to her cabin. I decided to bring her bring to my dorm room. It was only twenty feet away, she could sleep in my bed, which would be weird. I never really liked sleeping in a stranger's bed, mostly because of germs or comfort level or other imaginary things I would make up about the situation, but she was drunk and most likely completely blacked out. Her imagination wasn't working too hard.

I helped her down the hallway to my bedroom. I helped her into bed, put the pillow under her head. All the beds distributed by the canyon were the same, same bed, same pillows, same sheets, same everything. She felt comfortable and went to sleep.

I had to go to work in the morning. I took an extra sheet and a spare pillow from the closet and slept on the floor.

When I woke up in the morning Samantha was still there. She looked okay, she wasn't dead. She would live to experience more things and suffer more pain and fall in and out of love and watch *The Daily Show*. One day she would be old, sick with something terminal. She would die then.

Ice Cream Shack Condor

The ice cream shack was located in the Bright Angel complex. It faced the canyon, and there were big giant windows. You could cashier or scoop ice cream and look right onto the canyon. It was the best job I've ever had, if it paid at least $24,000 a year and offered reasonably good health insurance I would have done it for the rest of my life. It was the dream, some people wanted to be doctors or nurses or famous athletes, I wanted to work in the ice cream shop on the edge of the Grand Canyon. But there were several problems, number one, it was only open in the summer, and number two, it paid like eight something an hour with really no chance of a worthwhile raise. Even if a person has enough money to eat and drink beer, eventually life intrudes. You have to get your teeth repaired, you need to fix or buy a car. Something happens that demands a few thousand bucks. That job didn't offer it, it was the best job I ever had, but my life doesn't allow for such luxuries.

My job was to cashier and to sometimes scoop ice cream. I would go into the ice cream shack an hour before it opened and put out the mats and make sure everything was set up for the day. Our main concern was getting the ice cream from the freezer. The ice cream shack wasn't connected to the main hallway of the building. I would have to go with Rich, a big Navajo guy, and I mean he was big, he was so big they called him Bear. He was six-foot-five and built real strong, not overweight, just big and strong. He was quiet, he didn't speak unless he had something to say. He was young, about nineteen, and really awkward, but good at his job. He always showed up on time, his till was always perfect at the end of shift and the managers liked him. He had lived at the canyon almost five years, his mom got a job at the post office, which gave her a cheap house and a nice place to live, close enough to the reservation where she could visit home often and see her family.

To get the ice cream, Rich and I had to go inside the freezer all the way on the other side of the building. First we had to leave the ice cream shack and then walk around the building until we got to the Arizona style steakhouse and had to keep going until we got to the smoking area for employees. There were always people out there, usually the head manager Linda would be there smoking, talking about how her dad was in the military and how she needed to get things done. I actually liked her, she had to run four restaurants at once, there was no time for bullshit.

Rich and I would go into the freezer and get the ice cream, we threw the giant buckets of ice cream on a flat thing with wheels, then had to push it all the way back around the building. As we pushed the gallons and gallons of ice cream on the edge of the Grand Canyon, I would look over. You couldn't help looking over, there it was, the Grand Canyon. I felt lucky, like I had done the right things in life, that everything I had done up until then must have been true and right and strong if it had led me to that moment.

We got the ice cream inside and unloaded it.

Miss Teen Navajo was making the hot dogs, I ate so many of those hot dogs that summer, best hot dogs in America. Usually we would steal one and sit in the supply closet and eat one real quick before any managers noticed.

Miss Teen Navajo was named Ashley, she was eighteen and remarkable in her beauty. She'd grown up in Pima, Arizona and moved up to the canyon with her parents several years prior because her dad got a job working in the maintenance department and her mom was a manager of a hotel in Tusayan. Ashley made albums of

Navajo music. It was one of the reasons she had won Miss Teen Navajo. In order for you to win, you had to celebrate native culture and keep it alive. Ashley and Rich told me that Navajos had never joined the world of rock and rap music, they liked some of it, of course, who doesn't, and there were even rock and rap musicians amongst the native people, but they still believed in their traditional music. They still believed in their culture. I bought her album on a professional CD for $20. I listened to it in my car a few times.

Ashley would make hot dogs, Rich and I would be on the registers. There was also Debbie from the Bronx. She was a whirlwind of human emotion and eastern American sadness. She was born in Puerto Rico and moved to the Bronx as a little kid. She was short and curvy and her black hair was always slick looking and pulled back in strange designs. She was the shift manager of the ice cream shack and made maybe a quarter more than us. She would run around telling us to stop eating hot dogs and ice cream. We absolutely were never going to stop eating the hot dogs and ice cream. As soon as she went on a smoke break, we would immediately start eating hot dogs and ice cream. Free food was our main motivation for work.

Debbie had some bad things happen in her life, she was torn asunder. I was also torn asunder, but I had the privilege of growing up in a suburb with a good public school, and then attending college. I had a massive amount of student loans, but I was on the income-based repayment program. I never told them I had a job in Korea, which means they never knew I had any money. My tax returns said zero money earned, and I didn't even have to pay them either because I was so poor. I had loans but had at that point in my life never paid a dollar back to my grand debt.

Debbie was not as lucky as me, she grew up with Spanish-speaking parents who couldn't help her with her homework. No one she knew had ever gone to college. She was small and brown and had a slight accent, half her family was addicted to drugs and were constantly causing her problems. And then, a few years before I had met her, her mother was shot and killed. Her mother was dead, her father had left when she was a child, and her brother was in prison, she had had enough, she was working at a cheese store, selling gourmet cheese to rich people, when one of the customers told her about living at the Grand Canyon for a summer, "All you have to do is go online and apply, they hire everybody and since you have register and food and beverage experience, they will hire you for sure." Debbie, in her life of defeat, tears, and heartache, went online and found the company website. She filled out the application and a week later they emailed back saying she was hired, she took all the money she had and bought a plane ticket to Flagstaff. She had been working at the Grand Canyon for over six months and she said she had no plans on leaving.

The ice cream shop would open at 10am. Tourists would slowly start coming, in the morning they would mostly buy hot dogs and chips. The foreign tourists would hold out their hands full of change, and Rich and me would politely pick the correct coins out of their hands. I always smiled when I had to do that, making sure they knew it was okay, I understood memorizing America's system of currency was not the most important thing in the world.

Around 10:30 one morning a tourist came in and yelled, "There's a condor!"

There were barely any customers and the ones that were there got excited too. The customers and employees all ran outside, Rich, Debbie, Ashley and I. We left our stations of ice cream service and bolted to see the condor.

The sky was a light blue, with white fluffy clouds like broken up cotton above the north rim of the canyon. A giant condor, black with white underneath its wings, soared close above our heads.

There it was, I thought, the great California condor. There were only 400 or so left at that time, a rare bird fighting for survival. It was like a god floating in the ether, a power of its own, something left from another time, millions of years ago. Nature had forgotten to kill it, but it remained, and now it was slowly dying because of man's endless delusional needs.

I stood there with two Navajos, a person of African descent, tourists from Japan and Korea, a man and her husband from Italy, a woman wearing a hijab, tourists from Chile and Argentina, all witnessing the last remnants of the California condor. Why couldn't we get it together to save these animals? What was wrong with us? Why did North Americans, Europeans and East Asians have to cover everything with cement, malls, cities, why did we have to burn fossil fuels when we could all stand together, and look upon the condor together, with no sense of discrimination? At that moment, we weren't anything but humans witnessing and experiencing a giant bird, no religion, no race, just authentic human experience. I felt happiness because I had been so close to the giant condor, but I felt sadness because my species wanted to pillage the earth then take what they pillaged and turn it into garbage and toxins.

It might be possible that there is only one good planet in the whole system, I had been to the top of Colorado Rockies, I saw that no food grew there. With a deviation of 12,000 feet nothing grows. We had so much luck, the planet is magnetic and reflects solar flares, we have water and land, the planet isn't covered with ice, all of it isn't desert. But we are the planet, humans aren't separate from the planet, they are the planet, just like water that floods and destroys the land, humans are the same as a drought that kills animals, humans are the same as lightning that burns down a forest, humans are the same as a shark eating a school of fish, we aren't any different. Is that an excuse? I don't know. I went back to the ice cream shack.

After work I remembered the first time I saw a condor in 2000. I was walking along the same rim, the sun was setting Two teenage French girls pointed at a condor and said, "Le condor, le condor." I looked and saw a condor. I wondered if there were more or fewer of them then. Then I wondered about the French girls, they were in their late 20s then, they had been to college, started a career, maybe one of them had a baby and a nice husband, maybe one of them had a horrible breakup, she found her college boyfriend of several years cheating and could never love again. They were somewhere on the planet, probably worried about what would happen next.

After I saw the condor I sat next to the rim on some rocks near a couple in their 50s, they were healthy and strong-looking. They looked nothing like my parents or my friends' parents. The adults I grew up with were all overweight from an excessive amount of sugar consumption, they spent their days watching television and sports, they didn't exercise at gyms, ride bicycles or read books to relax. It was the first time I had seen American adults who looked like that. They started talking to me, they said they were from Northern California. The man said he made furniture for years, but then decided in his 40s to go to law school to fight for the environment. The woman said she was a schoolteacher but in her 40s switched to social work. I can never forget his face, it was handsome, strong and full of meaning and purpose. I wanted that face to be mine, I wanted to grow up and have a face that was strong with purpose. The face was also inviting too, it showed no signs of bitterness. This man didn't spend his days like my father, talking about women's asses and how the blacks at work wouldn't show up on time. Those types of discussions would never have crossed this man's mind, this man had different things on his mind.

The man said to me, "You are young, your life is like, as Dogen said 'A fish swims and never runs out of water, a bird flies but never runs out of air.' There is no end or beginning, different stages, but no end or beginning. There is no need to stop or go, no need for a verdict, no need to call it quits, no need to replicate. There is no solution that will solve your problems, you will never have a firm beautiful resolution, don't even seek it. Don't look for a solution, don't look for a resolution, you will never find it. You will have to live through your twenties now, if you are lucky and you might not be, you will have guidance in your life. There will be adults who help you. You will be loved and this love will guide you through college and then to a career. But to attain these things you will need guidance and love. If you have no guidance and love, then you will stumble, and the world will be a lonely place. You will never know where to direct yourself, because guidance is direction, guidance is a compass to safety. Some people have that compass and some people don't. It is needless to waste your time blaming yourself or others, never waste your time with blame. Don't even blame yourself, because you always have a chance to choose different things tomorrow. Go to sleep and move another direction tomorrow. You are beautiful and young now, your body is in good health, the world expects nothing of you, you are free. Because your life has no meaning, it will feel like, maybe you are a fish with too much water, a bird with too much air. Sometimes you realize you are going to die, and even though the end is decades away, it still feels threatening, overwhelming, a world with too much water. You will fall in love, maybe she will stay, maybe she won't. It might be your fault if she leaves, you have to accept it might be your fault. A future is coming, and you will be scared, it will come anyway. When it comes, it will just be more *now*. You will have a choice, to let your heart die, to let the child inside you die, or to keep it alive. Most let their heart die, some let it die when they are very young, some in their teens, very few hearts escape the twenties. Your heart, for it not to die, demands you keep surprising it. You have to keep waking it up with shocks and disruptions. Surprise is the key to this, fighting through fear, laughing at demons, even laughing at angels. Saying goodbye when you don't want to, saying hello when you don't want to, if you are not vigilant, you can ruin yourself. This is your life." The man pointed at the condor. "That is the life of the condor." He pointed at a Utah Juniper, "That is the life of that tree. It is not a requirement for you to get bored, to settle, to let your heart die. Your 30s will come and you will see that most of the things you worried about were trivial, nonsense, that they had no essential meaning. You won't even remember your worries, you will have new worries, but it isn't worries that ruin a life, it is the frustrations. If we let bitterness control us, frustrations will become our instinctual reactions. You won't have a mental paradigm that contains God, nature or ethical responsibility. You will have a mental paradigm of frustrations. If you make it out of your 30s without being consumed by mental frustrations, you will win a good 30 to 40 years of peace, glory, smiles, and cheerfulness."

I sat there, confused and said, "But what are these frustrations?"

The man smiled and said, "How many people in your life get angry when there is a long line, when the food doesn't come quickly at a restaurant, when they buy shoes that hurt their feet, when they get one pimple, when their hair doesn't look right, when someone has something they don't have. People who spend their days worried about other races, about what women are doing, how if they go to a park on the weekend there are too many people, how much food costs, how taxes are too high, how they can't get a good parking space, how much this cost and that cost, how they are right about heaven or not eating meat or about what music or movies are good, and everyone else is wrong. These people of frustration, they don't know it, but waiting in line, cleaning, riding in cars, sitting at restaurants, that's their life, that is exactly their life. Just as the condor hovers over us, hovering and looking for prey, just as the tree slowly grows over there, there is no difference. If you allow yourself to become infused with anger over the price of apples, over how other people drive cars, then your life will be anger. You will live for anger, anger for what you don't have, anger over what other people are doing, anger over the existence of other people, anger will be your guidance in life, anger will be your compass. You won't even know it, but anger will be your favorite emotion, and that will be your adult life. Your heart will die and anger will grow in its place."

I don't know why that man said those things. I stood up and walked back to my dorm.

Grandview Trail with Patricia

Patricia worked at the hotel in the Bright Angel building. At the end of my shift at the ice cream shop I had to put my till away in a lock box behind the hotel counter. We ended up talking and realized we had things in common. She was in her early 40s, and she loved hiking. She was Filipino, short, with long black hair. She had put some weight on, she had the body of a woman, she was not a child, didn't feel insecure. She had suffered and had unseen scars.

Patricia had grown up in the Philippines, she never specified where. She was always silent on her early life in the Philippines. She said she had a mother there, but had no interest in visiting the Philippines, it had been 17 years since she'd last seen her homeland. This was incredible to me, because when I was in Korea I wanted deeply at times to go home. I missed people badly, but she missed no one. I would often lie in my bed and daydream about talking to certain friends, about being in America and eating American foods, about what I would say to people, about what they would say to me, about how wonderful it would be to be at home. But she felt nothing, she had no desire to go home. I realized even though I came home, I was not at home in the Midwest. I wasn't talking to anyone from Ohio. I was at the Grand Canyon, doing what I had always done, traveling, keeping on the move, using travel as a way to bolster my self-esteem. When I was in Korea, I could tell myself, "I am in Korea, I am doing something with my life." I would post pics of myself on Facebook and people I went to high school and college with would see them and think, "Billy is doing something great. He is living in Korea." Now I was at the Grand Canyon. I was posting pics, asking everyone to think thoughts about me, asking people I didn't even talk to, people I didn't truly care about, to think positive thoughts about me. They were having babies and I was hiking with sad Filipino women. Do the people on Facebook know I cry sometimes, that I miss someone, that I stare at jackrabbits asking for hope, asking jackrabbits to change me, to alter my mind, to make these recurring thoughts fall out of my head? I began to wonder if the sad thoughts could end, if they would ever complete themselves, resolve themselves. If the sad thoughts would ever walk away from me, like she did.

Sometimes, I would imagine holding her hand. I could even feel her hand in my hand, I would look down and her little hand would be in mine. Sometimes I could trick myself into thinking it was real, having the true textural feeling of her hand.

Patricia had similar problems. She had an imaginary hand she would hold.

Patricia and I decided to hike Grandview Trail together. I had not hiked with anyone in a long time. I didn't know what would happen, but I hoped for the best.

I woke up at 5 a.m., showered and walked to the coffee shop. The coffee shop was really just the Bright Angel bar, but in the mornings, they served cappuccino and pastries instead of alcohol. I loved that part of Bright Angel, it was full of old logs, beautiful paintings of Hopis, and smelled so polite and charming. I got a hot coffee and went to Victor Hall to wait for Patricia.

I sat on the ground cross-legged, I felt happy that morning, the sun was rising, the air was soft. A group of mule deer stood by eating grass. It seemed as if the mule deer never stopped eating.

Patricia finally arrived 20 minutes late. I didn't say anything when I got in the car. She was holding a coffee too.

She immediately started, "Okay, I've done this trail. I did this trail with a guy two years ago, I met him on a website. It was a dating website, I didn't know what I was doing on the website, but my husband died, did I tell you that? My husband died. We were married for ten years, and like, I loved him. I felt, I was finally happy, I was happy. I thought God loved me. When we were married he told me, 'I waited for 30 years to meet you, when I met you, it felt like my life started, it felt like the earth was not the earth anymore, but a new planet, a planet I could live on, when I looked in the mirror, my own face looked different, when I felt your body, your body changed me, I will never leave you, because there is no me without you. If I for some reason was without you, I would no longer be myself. I would be a different person, a lesser person.' That's what he told me when we got married. Then one day nine years after our marriage, our perfect union, he came home from the doctor and said he had cancer. He told me he had cancer, I couldn't believe him. How could he leave me? But he did, he left me. I watched him die. I watched the man I loved grow weaker and weaker. I watched him eat less and less, I sat by his bed and read him books, we watched his favorite movies. I was stupidly convinced he would get better, that I would wake up and go into his room and he would be better. I often had dreams of him being better, I still do. I still dream of him, in all the dreams his body works, he eats, and wants to spend time with me. Well, that is what happened, he died. I didn't understand what happened, can you forgive me? I hope he forgives me, but I went on a dating site shortly after and met a rich man. He had a lot of money, he paid for my ticket to the Grand Canyon. I didn't care, I wanted affection, I had affection for a decade and then it was gone, I had a body next to me for ten years, I had the hands of a man on my body for ten years, but then, no more. What was I supposed to do? Tell me, there was nothing I could do, I went to the Grand Canyon with a rich man who would buy me a ticket, who bought me camping gear and hiking shoes. He bought me things. I met him at the Grand Canyon, he wanted me to be happy, I didn't care about being happy, I wanted to stop the pain, I went to the Grand

Canyon, me and the man went down Grandview Trail, we spent the night in a tent, had bad sex. It was like tent sex, tent sex is never good. But when I woke up, when I left the tent, I stood outside the tent on the Horseshoe Mesa, I knew I was not in love with the man in the tent. The man in the tent was nothing to me, the Grand Canyon was my home. I had to get back to the Grand Canyon, it was calling me, I could hear it, it was speaking to me, it said, 'Patricia, come, I will heal you.' I believed the canyon, I really believe the canyon calls us. It is like a beacon or something, a lighthouse, a force that wants certain people to come to its power. I believe if you have pain, you can give it to the Grand Canyon, the canyon will take it, I believe that."

She didn't ask me to believe that, she didn't ask me anything. It was like her emotions couldn't be controlled anymore. She had to be vulnerable, she had to get it out, she had to release it. All my life, people would get me alone and confess their life. People felt safe to be vulnerable around me, I would listen, and not judge. That was my talent, not judging. I didn't have a philosophical reason for not judging, I never cared, but I did something even weirder, I never justified good or bad behavior, I didn't say, "Well, she's a horrible person because she has so much anxiety, she can't help it," or, "He's a great person because he really loves people," or, "He can't help it, he's a product of his environment." None of those sentences seemed true to me. Truths always seemed like trying to hold water, you can't hold water, you can't hold truth. Nowhere in the universe was one truth located, there was always this incredible thing happening, it seemed ridiculous having those thoughts, having deep thoughts. I was only having deep thoughts to distract myself from the fact I would never talk to her again.

We arrived at the trailhead, she parked her SUV and we filled our water bottles. She pulled out a large digital camera. I looked at the camera and felt scared. People always brought cameras on hikes and took a million pictures, I don't even know if they ever looked at the pictures. Someone who took a lot of pictures told me once that he did look at the pictures, that he would sit alone in his room at the computer editing and shuffling them around for hours while listening to his favorite music. He would sit and smile and look at pictures of past events, moments that would never happen again.

At the beginning of a trail you've never done before, you don't know what will happen. You looked at pictures on Google image search, but those pictures didn't have the answers. Those pictures never told you how much your feet and legs would hurt or what animals you would see. You have to let yourself follow the trail. The trail controls you, it dictates your movements. The trail gives you the magic, you don't bring magic to the trail.

As we were hiking down the trail I asked Patricia, "How did you get to America? Did you have a relative here?" I asked this innocently, I had never known anyone from the Philippines that came to America in the 90s.

She replied, "It was by pen pal." I kept hiking without saying anything, my brain worked through the phrase 'pen pal.' What does 'pen pal' mean? Oh my god, it hit me, she was a mail order bride, I was hiking with a real mail order bride. All my life up until that point, I had made fun of men from America who had mail order brides. They were the butt of jokes, funny funny ha ha mail order bride. But there was one, right in front of me, a mail order bride.

Patricia continued, "I was married to some guy for three years, it was stupid. It was like, just dumb, I didn't love the man. He had a good job and he tried to be nice, but there was nothing to him, there was nothing sexual about him. He moved so awkwardly, he sat awkwardly, he went to the bathroom awkwardly, his voice was even awkward. He would sit and say, 'Patricia, you are so beautiful, the most beautiful girl in the world.' Then he would move his hand slowly out and touch my arm. There was no smoothness to him, I never felt emotions for him. I would tell him I loved him, he knew I didn't love him. We would eat dinner and watch TV together at the beginning, but eventually I would eat alone and spend hours in my room by myself. He knew I was going to leave, it made him sad. He would sit for hours in a reclining chair watching television with this sad—I hate to say it—a stupid look on his face. Yeah, the look on his face was stupid. Sometimes I think about that stupid look and just get angry. When he would fart I would get so angry, the way he used a fork even made me scream at the end. When it was time I left, I said goodbye, and I haven't spoken to him since."

Then we stopped at a pretty rock. It was a big red boulder, she wanted to climb on it and get her picture taken. She taught me how to use her camera, it wasn't hard, just press a button. She told me, "Don't put the focal point in the middle." She showed me lines on the camera where I should put her. Patricia climbed on top of the rock and stood strong, she made a face and said, "Take the picture, don't put me in the middle."

I looked at the screen on the camera and placed her on the right line and clicked the button. She yelled, "Keep taking more." I kept snapping photos, after each click she moved her body into a different pose. She really liked posing for the camera. I felt like laughing, I had the desire to make fun of her for it, but then I was like, no, she seems happy, let her be happy. I remained silent and did what she told me to with a small smile on my face.

As we walked down, one photo after another was taken, she was constantly stopping and having me take her photo. She took my photo a few times and told me she would send me the photos, but I have yet to see them, and I'm sure I never will.

When we got to Horseshoe Mesa I really liked it. It was this weird piece of flat land where no flat land should have been. We walked around for a long time. There was an old miner's cabin, there was nothing left but the stone walls. I went inside and looked around, I daydreamed about being a miner working in the Grand Canyon, about having a mule, giving the mule a name like Betsy or George. George the mule sounded really good, I didn't tell Patricia about my mule dreams.

Patricia didn't care about the cabin, she didn't seem to have any mule dreams. I started to wonder if she had a mule in the Philippines, if she and her grandfather had to feed the mule together. If her grandfather told her funny jokes, if her grandfather had a funny nickname for her. I wondered about her sweating as a child in the Philippines, but what she did I would never know, she had no interest in telling me stories about that place.

We walked over to the campground, there were no tents, no one was there, not one warm ember on any of the fire pits. There was a weird outhouse that was elevated and in the open air, it had special things inside it that would eat the poop, it said to throw nothing but paper inside.

I walked over to Patricia and she said, "That's where our tent was."

"When you stayed with the man from the Internet?"

"Yeah, I had sex right there," she pointed at a spot on the ground.

"You have a good memory," I said while looking at the spot imagining her having sex in a tent with a man with a very good job.

"I didn't love him either, I once loved a man and he died. Let's go to the caves."

Patricia told me there were caves on the edge of the Horseshoe Mesa, they were called Caves of the Domes. I didn't bother to Google Caves of the Domes, I had no idea what she was talking about.

We walked and walked around the age of the Mesa, but found nothing. I was starting to worry that it was taking up too much time and we wouldn't get home till after dark, and I didn't have a flashlight or a coat, because after it gets dark it immediately gets cold at the Grand Canyon.

While looking for the Caves of the Domes I walked straight into a Yucca plant, the sharp leaf went straight into my leg. I felt pain for a few seconds, then looked down and my leg was bleeding a good amount. Dark red blood left my body, flowing over my leg hair. I didn't care, it seemed beautiful to me, this blood, I wanted to shed blood. I told Patricia, "Look, I'm bleeding." She walked over to me and said, "You're fine, keep walking." Patricia was not the usual woman I would hang out with. Everyone I ever dated would have taken a photo and made jokes about vampires or sacrificing blood to the canyon. She said nothing, she had other things on her mind, caves, she had to get to the caves.

After I cut myself and bled for the gods, the gods were nice enough to lead us to the caves.

We stood at the entrance to the caves, Patricia pulled out her flashlight and shined a light in. Dust particles. Millions of dust particles. I looked at all the dust particles and remembered I had allergies and this wasn't a great place for people with allergies to go, but I knew Patricia was not going to take no for an answer. I took my bandana from my bag and wrapped it around my face and said, "Let's go."

We entered the cave slowly, there wasn't much to see except dust particles, a few times my arm hit Patricia's arm, it almost seemed romantic but Patricia never acknowledged it. There wasn't even an, "Oh, I'm sorry." I immediately forgot our arms ever touched, obviously it was about the caves.

We slowly walked deeper and deeper in the caves, but there wasn't anything in there, just more cave and dust particles. Patricia said, "You want to get out of here?" I replied, "Yeah, it is just caves of dust."

We left the dusty caves and walked back outside, the air felt clean. I felt grimy, the grimy feeling never left for the rest of the hike. It felt like dust was everywhere, even my eyelashes felt full of dust, I put my hand in my hair and dust fell out, and when I looked down at the blood on my leg, the dark red blood was full of dust.

We walked back up the trail, the way up a trail always goes faster. Patricia wanted to walk alone, she moved her feet very slowly. She told me she loved the canyon and did not want to leave it, she knew it was calling her. She told me that the canyon would take her pain, she said, "Give it to the canyon, give your pain to the canyon, it'll take it." I believed her.

We saw a giant jackrabbit, it was the biggest jackrabbit I had ever seen. I yelled, "Patricia, do you see that jackrabbit?" She responded, "Yes."

Kaja

A week before things got weird between me and Kaja, I went to her cabin with Maszov and some beers. We stayed up late talking, eventually Maszov got mad and left. Maszov liked Kaja, Kaja felt fine with Maszov but did not like him like that. Maszov felt stupid for introducing me to Kaja, maybe Maszov assumed I would have liked Marcelina. Maszov's calculations were wrong.

After Maszov left, Marcelina wanted to go to sleep. The cabin was open, two beds in one room, and one tiny bathroom. She put on a cute eye cover, pulled the blankets over her and curled up in bed waiting for me to leave. But it was obvious to me that Kaja wanted to keep talking to me, I felt really enthusiastic about talking to Kaja and didn't want to stop. I remembered my roommate was at his girlfriend's dorm room in Colter Hall, and asked Kaja if she wanted to come back to my room. I don't know why I asked her that, it caused a lot of anxiety, I kept asking myself, "Why am I bothering this person?" Then I would ask myself, "Why do I even have emotions?" Then I would tell myself, "Please stop having emotions, they aren't helping you. You need to be figuring out what to do with your life."

Kaja said yes.

I was surprised. Kaja got a flashlight, put on a little black jacket that was so European. I couldn't imagine an American woman ever wearing a jacket like that.

To get back to Victor Annex we had to walk over the train tracks. We walked together through the night, I wanted to hold her hand, I wanted to feel her little hand in mine. I could see her small hands popping out the sleeves of her black European jacket, but her hands were not touching mine, I wanted those hands.

We crossed the tracks together. We kept finding things to laugh about, she kept telling me not to step on mule or elk poop. She loved making mule poop jokes. I asked why she made so many mule poop jokes, she replied, "I am mule poop expert." I would laugh hysterically at this. We were two silly people, one person with a master's degree, one trilingual person with a bachelor's, making poop jokes in the night.

When we got to my room, it was boring. I had nothing in my room, no television, no radio, no cool computer to watch movies on. I was such an idiot, it was obvious that I was trying to do something creepy, I was being creepy. I realized I was being creepy and almost hated myself, but since I am a guy, and creepiness seems written into our genetic code, I only mildly felt stupid.

Kaja and I sat three feet apart on the bed talking for a long time. She told me she had a brother and he went to school, that she lived with him in Poznan. Her father owned a business, he worked long hours. They were okay, he had always been there for her, he had never said anything mean, he was just very consumed with working. She said, "He is like, duty dad, is that how you say?"

"Well, I've never said it like that, but I understand, you mean, like, he thinks it is duty to provide money and shelter, not so much affection."

"Hmm, yes, but affection, what do you mean?"

"Like hugging, laughing with you, going places with you, talking about feelings."

"Yes, he never talk about feelings. My mother sometimes talks about feelings."

"Does your brother?"

"When he was younger, but now, he wants money and hardly ever talks about feelings," she said.

Then she told me about how she lived in Spain, that she loves Spain and America, and even England. That one time when she was little, her family went to Tunis. Her dad always wanted to experience a Muslim country and got a good deal on the tickets. She said she loved it and thought it was a beautiful place. Honestly, I kind of expected her to say something bad about Muslims, being from Poland, and basing things off what I heard on the news. But she never said anything mean about anyone. Kaja would say, "Everyone is same." I would reply, "But there are cultural differences," and she would reply, "Everyone is same." She didn't have a grand theory on why everyone was the same, as far as she would go was, "I've been to several countries, everyone is same."

While she talked, I kept thinking, try to kiss, ask her if she wants to kiss you. My mind became very obsessive with these thoughts, it was obnoxious. There was no reason to bring kissing into the moment, all we were doing was talking about our parents. How can talking about our parents make kissing reasonable?

I stopped talking and waited a minute and said, "Can I kiss you?" I always asked this before I kissed someone. Kaja said no, she didn't want to kiss me. She had a goofy look on her face, maybe she wanted to wait a few days, maybe she just wanted to be friends, maybe she felt nervous about other things, things I would have never guessed. I allowed all those ideas to take place.

She stood up and I walked her home over the train tracks.

A few days later I went to the grocery store, and bought two jars of peanut butter, one for her and one for Marcelina. Every time I buy a surprise gift for someone I always feel scared and dumb, like

89

what am I doing? Is this really what other people want? I bought the peanut butter.

I knocked on Kaja's door that night holding the peanut butter, she opened the door looking at me. She had no specific emotion on her face, she told me to sit. I sat down on the bed and handed her the peanut butter, she became excited holding the peanut butter. She opened it up and scooped some out and started laughing. Seeing her laugh made me feel better, I wasn't the stupidest creepiest asshole ever.

We talked about work and our coworkers. I think we also talked about pizza.

After we talked for a half an hour I went back to Victor Annex, I got a warm beer and sat outside smoking cigarettes with Dream. He told me about how a server dropped a whole tray of prepared food at the El Tovar in an elevator.

Two days after giving Kaja the peanut butter I saw her in Maswik Cafeteria. We sat together and ate burritos made by people from Romania and Taiwan. Making chicken burritos was intense cultural immersion for the Romanians and Taiwanese. You would say, "cilantro" and instead of putting a normal amount, they would hold it, looking at it, wondering about what it was, smell it, think about the cilantro, then throw on way too much. Then they would scoop up the beans, puzzle over the beans, question the existence of pinto beans themselves, and then throw way too little on, you ended up with a burrito of cilantro with one half full spoon of beans. In Korea I was lucky I had never had to make food. I don't know what I would have done if I got off the plane in Korea and I had to make jjajangmyeon or dukbokki, I tried to make dukbokki when I came home from Korea to my parents' house, it was horrible. I felt bad for the Romanians and Taiwanese and their burrito lives.

I got my badly made burrito and walked into the cafe. Kaja was sitting at a table by herself, I smiled at her, she smiled at me, she waved me over. I think I might have been crazy, I shouldn't have walked over there, I should have sat by Rich from the ice cream shack. Rich saw me, and I waved but pointed at Kaja. Rich shook his head smiling. If I sat next to Rich I would have been safe, Rich didn't care about entangling me, he usually talked about mountain lions or his brother who moved to Fresno.

I sat down across from Kaja, I smiled, she looked at me, she smiled. There it was, the weird nature of romance, two people, one from the bottomless pit of industrial Ohio, and the other from Poland. She would go back to Poland, she would return to the snow, to the 500-year-old buildings, she would return to her beautiful city. I had no intention of loving her, I had no intention of marrying her, but she wanted to be nice to me, and no one had been nice to me in a long time.

When I first met her, she was wonderful. I met her in a small apartment by a college campus, her friends were there, her friend had a pet snake, she wrapped the small python around her neck and laughed. A month later, we went outside after a few drinks, and she did gymnast tumbles in the snow, wearing a winter coat. I fell in love with her. I wanted a woman that tumbled, I did not know I wanted such a woman, but I guess I did. When I was sick, she would make me soup. When I had a skin rash, she didn't make fun of me, she put creams softly on my body. We traveled to Maine together, we ate lobster, lobster soup, lobster hot dogs, and lobster mac 'n cheese. We made love, we made love all night, a thousand positions, our hands grasping tight, her butt in my hands, her hands on my biceps, her eyes looking up into mine, my eyes looking down into hers. One time I came into her bedroom on a balmy summer evening, she was naked in her bed, lying on her tummy, her beautiful little butt open to the air. When did the sex end? When did I do or say the wrong thing that led to her feeling that sex with me was a negative? At some moment, I must have done the wrong thing. Sometimes when I was walking around the canyon, I would make a list of all the possible things I could have done wrong. I told myself, "Billy, don't ever do those things again, stop hurting other people, stop hurting yourself." She was nice to me for a long time.

When we were in Korea, I protected her, I felt like a real man for the first time in my life. I took her garbage out, I helped clean the apartment, I gave her money when she needed it. I would buy her cute things, she would smile. I was like my grandfather, a real man, a man that went to work and bought things for a woman. My grandfather was more masculine than me. He watched sports, he could fix cars, he could put on roofs and construct shelves. He could kill a deer, gut it and carry it back to the cabin. He had a lawn he mowed perfectly, the grass never got so high it seeded. My grandfather took stinky shits because he ate red meat and consumed cheap beer. He went to work and did his job, he had a duty to be a man, he had a commitment to being a man, to having a wife, to having kids, and he did not break it. Where was my manhood? Where was my lawn full of grass that needed to be mowed? I didn't have any of that, I had a relationship that had no longer justified itself. Then it was all blood and guts, a bunch of ugly that would not relent. I have told no one about this ugliness, she hasn't either. She would be too embarrassed, I too am embarrassed, and I tell everyone everything. But I can't speak of what happened, sometimes I hear songs, the saddest songs, and I hear what happened in the notes, in the chords, the lyrics don't say it, but I know what happened to the singer, I know what happened to the piano player, to the guitar player. I can see them wandering the night, looking for someone they can't find.

I sat down at the cafeteria table in Maswik, looking at Kaja, knowing all these facts. Knowing my heart was torn asunder. That my ability to trust, to leap into romance, to forgive, was not there.

Kaja said to me, "Do you like pets?"

I replied, "When I was growing up, we only had chickens and rabbits."

She laughed and said, "Chickens and rabbits, no dogs or cats?"

"No, my mother wouldn't let us have indoor pets. To fix this problem my dad had outdoor pets, he built a chicken coop in the backyard and a rabbit cage. He usually had four hens and two roosters. Well, there were two roosters until the one rooster we called Roody killed the other rooster. Roody was horrible, I hated that rooster."

"You named the rooster what?"

"Roody," I said slowly.

She said, "Roody," back.

"Well, Roody hated me. When I was walking around the yard, the rooster would attack me with its huge claws. It was terrible, I would scream, I was constantly under attack by that damn rooster."

Kaja laughed.

I continued, "In the winter it would be really cold, there would be snow and ice. I would have to feed the chickens, I had to walk up on the hill wearing my dad's giant boots and a thick winter coat. Their water would be frozen, I'd have to break the ice out of it and pour in the hot water. No matter how cold it got, the chickens didn't die, the freezing temperatures didn't bother them at all. Did you have any pets?"

She smiled and said, "Yes, my family has always had dogs. When we were growing up we had a little dog, I don't know what the word for it is in English. I would cuddle the dog at night, I would talk to the dog for hours about musicians and movie characters I liked. The dog never responded, the dog only listened. My father didn't like the dog, he would hide from it. Everyone would make fun of my dad for not loving the dog. If the dog was sitting in my dad's chair, he would look like he was going to cry. He would ask me or my brother to get the dog out of his chair, he would never touch it. One day the dog got cancer. Shortly after, it died. My brother has a dog now, when I am in Poland I have dog. But the dog sleeps in my brother's bed, not mine."

We finished our food and walked back to Kaja's cabin, she invited me. She handed me a piece of gum and said, "Take this."

I took the gum and began to chew it.

Kaja sat on the bed and motioned me over. I should have left, went back to my room and read a book about Buddhism, found spiritual enlightenment, listened to my headphones, took a nap. But no, I was about to get in a bed with a young Polish woman. I felt at times the Grand Canyon was controlling me, bringing me to places, whether I wanted to go there or not. I could not fight the canyon, I had to do what the canyon wanted.

We sat next to each other on the bed, she gave me that look women give when they are ready to be kissed, I could see it, there it was, the look. I put my arm around her and kissed her, she slightly opened her mouth. Her wet tongue touched my wet tongue.

We laid down on the bed, our bodies touching. Her arms around me, my arms around her, her legs tangled up in mine. There was no sex, only hugging, kissing, not even a grope. It was like I returned to that basement in 1996 when I first kissed Candace Delaney. Candace and I had beautiful make out sessions on an old seventies couch next to a pool table, and the water heater. Candace has three kids now and lives in a trailer in the same town where I grew up. My parents see her at the grocery store sometimes. My parents would never see Kaja, they would never know Kaja ever existed in my life.

After we were done kissing, I sat on the edge of the bed, I kept thinking the phrase, "Blood and guts in Korea, blood and guts at the canyon, blood and guts in Poznan. I don't have one friend in this whole world, blood and guts."

4th of July

On July 4th, the employee cafeteria was soon to close. There were no fireworks at the Grand Canyon, I didn't have to worry about rushing off to those. Mopping the floor; in my mind I remembered not seeing fireworks for five years. The last time I saw them was with her sitting on grass in a campus town. I don't know if we loved America that night, but we did, for real, love each other that night.

But my mind kept going further back into time. It ended up at the Grand Canyon, the year 2000. When I was at the canyon the first time I lived in Victor Hall, and rarely ever left it, I spent my life on that porch and in the TV room. I was good and drunk that night on 4th of July, a guy in his 30s named Neal bought me some beer. We all sat in the TV room, a bunch of guys, going late into the night celebrating a dream called America. I'm going to try to remember that night, our minds blur things, we know this, but I'm going to slip back into history, the time machine will take me there, I'll arrive and know that TV room again.

A bunch of guys sat in the TV room, there was a white guy in his thirties, slightly overweight, always wore the most unfashionable clothes. He had a funny French looking mustache and told us once, "Every time I look at the canyon, it is a different canyon." There was this bumbling white guy from Texas, who told us one night (all the secrets were revealed in that TV room) his father was gay, that when he came out as gay, chairs were thrown, the family splintered into divisions, but he still loved his father. There were two Mormon guys, they had grown up in Utah, they couldn't hack being Mormon. They wanted to drink, they didn't want to pay the church fee, they had other things they wanted to do, but they still respected the church, they still believed in the Miracle of the Gulls, they told us the story of the gulls that saved those pilgrims, and we all believed. I don't know where

97

those guys are, somewhere in America. Maybe some are dead, maybe some got their lives together and have kids and respectable jobs in Idaho or Florida, maybe some are standing on a corner somewhere picking up cigarette butts, and they are so tired they don't even wonder anymore.

There was an older Navajo in there that night, his name was Charles. On most nights when he came in the TV room, he wouldn't talk. He sat wearing blue jeans, an old t-shirt and a baseball cap with one feather on it. Growing up in Ohio a feather had always meant warrior. I would think about his feather, I had no feather, and I knew I would never get one.

On the 4th of July, 2000, Charles started talking, he was sitting next to another older Navajo, who kept quiet the entire time. When Charles commenced he couldn't stop. He told us he had fought in Vietnam. When I was growing up, Vietnam was still alive in the cultural consciousness, people still made movies about it, teenage boys loved to say "in Nam." The adults would mention Vietnam, how an uncle came back and was never the same, how they remembered the Tet Offensive, how their friends went off to war, how they went off to war, how they protested the war, it was real, it was mentioned. But it has been a long time since 2000, and no one mentions Vietnam anymore. We mention Fallujah, we mention our cousin who came back from Afghanistan who never gets off the couch because crowds make him cry, we mention our coworkers who are weird from the war. A new war happened, with new sad, mangled warriors.

Charles was from an older war, a war in Vietnam. He was happy at the beginning, it got him out of the desert, it got him money, a nice uniform, he had a sincere sense of pride. He kept saying, "I was young and this is what I thought." He didn't add to it, he didn't judge his young thoughts and feelings, he had them, and that was all. He said they sent him to Vietnam, and he felt scared, but truly, he didn't think he would see combat, it had never occurred to him that he would have to kill people or people were going to try to kill him.

Charles told us that he saw American planes bomb a village. The village, as in, the houses and everything they used to make their lives possible, caught on fire. After the fires started he and his fellow troops ran into the village. Charles, the man with the feather on his cap, said he saw burning babies, that living babies were on fire. When I was young and heard Charles say "burning babies" I thought it was terrifying, but I didn't truly imagine it, I didn't truly understand the implications of a human being lit on fire. But there, years later, after visiting Cambodia, having a very clear idea what Southeast Asian people look like, what Southeast Asia itself looks and feels like, after experiencing the people of Southeast Asia reading their histories, literature and folktales, I could really see that burning baby, I could see that village on fire.

Charles told us, and I don't how much of what he told was true, but this is what he said: He told us that he walked off in the middle of the night from the troop. He walked until he found Vietnamese people, he introduced himself the best he could, and started to live with them. If Charles really did this, it seems incredible now, looking back on it, was it courage that led him to walk alone in the jungle? Or had he gone mad from the burning baby?

Eventually Charles made it back to the American military, he never told us what happened after that.

I think I asked him questions, but it seems absurd to think about that image, seeing a 19-year-old white boy from Ohio ask stupid questions to an older Navajo man who saw burning babies in Vietnam. I'm an idiot.

Soon after Charles finished, he went to bed. I don't even think he told anyone goodnight. When everyone else began talking, he slipped out of the room.

As the night wore on, everyone had left the TV room except for a few of us. Martinez Whitehair remained in the room, he was a Hopi and in his later twenties. He washed dishes in one of the cafeterias. He was really weird, he wore his socks up to his knees, big converse sneakers, cut off blue jeans, a white t-shirt, and a netted red baseball cap, no memory of what the cap said, but there were definitely words on it.

Everyone was drunk, I was on my tenth beer, and had thrown down a few shots from a bottle of bourbon somebody was passing around. Martinez Whitehair told us that the language of the Hopis came from jackrabbits, their facial expressions came from yucca plants, their songs came from the love songs of birds. They had learned family life from mountain lions, and when hummingbirds came to you, they were sent by the gods, and if you could stop listening to the funny stubborn ideas in your head, you could hear the hummingbird speak. The hummingbird only gave the most painful directions, but if you did what the hummingbird told you to do, if you did not relent when everything told you to give up, you would know how to live, and those who were visited by a hummingbird were very lucky.

Shufen and Desert View

The Grand Canyon called Shufen, the canyon could hear her howl from Taiwan, her lonesome moan in the Taipei night. I could never figure out what Shufen was, was she a ghost, a mystic forest creature, the canyons and mountains of this world coming alive in one human body, or just a strong young woman who wanted to hike the trails of this earth? The world doesn't deserve people like Shufen, but the world needs people like Shufen.

I met Shufen in the employee cafeteria. A group of Taiwanese came up from Bright Angel Trail, they had hiked from one rim to the other, spending two nights in the canyon. They were all sweaty and disheveled, their feet were blistered, their eyes red with sweat, they were tired, but excited for what they had done. I went over and asked them about it, they told me they had gone to the other rim, they said in jumbled English that they had slept at the bottom.

But they didn't really want to talk, they were hungry and wanted to eat. But one of them started talking to me, she said her name was Shufen. She sat at the end of the table, she seemed alone, the others weren't really talking to her. She started telling me about the hike, which eventually led to me telling her about how I had been to the bottom earlier in the summer and had hiked on every day off, that I even went to Sedona. She told me she had done some trails, but she was alone, and none of the other Taiwanese friends wanted to hike that much. I told her that I would hike with her, she seemed really happy. A smile came on her face. She told me she didn't have a phone but she would come back and talk to me. I told her I usually work in the evening.

The next night Shufen came to visit me at the employee cafeteria, she would come wearing hiking gear, because that's all she

101

wore. I was surprised when she came back, a lot of people told me they wanted to hike with me, but they never mentioned it again, it happened almost every day.

I stood up from my stool at the register and said, "Hello Shufen. How are you?"

She stood there smiling, she pulled a bunch of papers out of her backpack. She said, "Billy, I can't read, Billy, you read."

"Okay," I said smiling.

She handed me the papers, we went over to a table and sat down. I looked at them and they said something about housing and beds, I said to her, "Shufen, it is okay, no need to worry."

"Worry?"

"Don't worry, don't think about."

She nodded and smiled.

"Do you want anything to eat?" I said.

She shook her head no.

"Was work okay?"

"Today very busy, I work a lot. But it okay."

Then she stood up, said bye and left.

Shufen would visit me almost every night. She would go to the ranger speeches, every night the rangers gave a half an hour speech on something about the park, Shufen would attend as many of those as possible, always by herself. I asked if she understood what the ranger was saying, and she replied that she understood some of it. Then she said, "There are videos, and pictures, I can look."

One day she invited me to see Desert View, Mary Colter's tower on the edge of the canyon. Shufen and I didn't have cars, a middle-aged woman named Robin drove us. Robin was Mormon and worked with Shufen in housekeeping. On the way to Desert View we stopped at the Tusayan Ruins, 800-year-old ruins made by the Pueblos. There was a little museum, it was weird, all the pictures of natives looked like white people.

While we were in the museum Robin told me her son was attacked by the curse of skinwalkers. Earlier in my life, I was a George Carlin/Dawkins kind of guy, I would have scoffed, maybe even told her she was dumb to her face. But I started to feel the world was a little X-Files. I didn't have a good reason for it, I didn't think George Carlin/Richard Dawkins had good reasons, I couldn't find any good or bad reasons anymore, I don't think I even cared about reasons anymore. I looked at Robin, and said, "Wait, what happened?"

Robin said, that her son was driving through the Navajo Reservation, when he was at a gas station a young Navajo man asked him for a ride to the next town. Robin's son said, "No, I don't think I can do that." Robin expressed, "I don't want my son picking up hitchhikers, you know, he's my son, and my son knows this, he's a good boy." The woman loved her son.

Robin went on, she said he was driving down the highway, and this thing, that looked like a person was running as fast as a car next to him. He kept looking at it, he felt terrified, he didn't know what it was. He was driving 70 miles an hour through the desert, how could something be running as fast as his car? The thing disappeared, but then it came back, it did it three more times until he left the reservation.

Then her son was plagued with bad luck for the next year, he had to find a Navajo shaman to lift the curse. I didn't ask her how being Mormon and believing in skinwalkers worked, but then, I thought, the X-Files don't care about what you tell yourself. Maybe there are X-Files, and they are happening all the time, but we are too busy worrying about if people like us, credit ratings, our hair, school assignments and in general all the dumb thoughts we are having cloud us from noticing cool things like skinwalkers, talking hummingbirds and when the Gods send us a friend named Shufen.

I walked among the 800-year-old ruins, circles made out of rocks. Shufen danced among the ruins, her eyes were big and she smiled. I have no idea what she was thinking, don't even want to guess. I didn't have any great thoughts looking at those stones piled in neat circles, everyone who made those stones were long dead. I was standing there, and one day, I would be long dead. Maybe that wasn't it, that wasn't the answer, the thought I was trying to have, because I was trying to have a thought. The thought that came was that when those people built those stone structures, they never knew that they would be turned into a tourist site. Everyone building those stone structures had ideas about the future, there were some people in their tribe that predicted all kinds of events, people who thought they knew everything and had no self-doubt. They knew what would happen for a thousand years, just like we have people who know what is going to happen in a thousand years. But I bet there were a few weird people, they didn't know what was going to happen, and when the predictors gave their amazing opinions, there was somebody that rolled their eyes, shook their head and said, "Really?" But there are always more predictors and controllers than eye-rollers.

We went on to Desert View, where the park ends and becomes the Navajo Reservation. We parked in the giant parking lot, it reminded me of an amusement park. We were a few hundred yards

104

away from the rim, we saw the tower Mary Colter built. They say Mary Colter demanded every stone had to be perfect, she believed in the canyon. Mary Colter was a true genius, she knew she would only have one chance to make this view of the canyon perfect, that the canyon demanded perfection. The canyon demands honor, it demands greatness from those who hike and live alongside it. The canyon has no interest in weakness or forgiveness. I imagined some of the workers taking a break on the edge of the canyon saying, "Oh hell, why won't Mary leave us alone!" And someone else saying, "Look at that canyon, it will be forever, whatever we do here, will last forever, a million eyes will see this tower, it has to be done right," and the other man nodding in agreement. The canyon demanded this beautiful structure, and Mary Colter knew that. She knew she had genius inside her, she knew the workers had genius inside them, she knew the rushing water of the Colorado was the true genius, and the power of the rushing Colorado lived inside her, and this ferocity and glory inside could be unleashed from within her.

We got to the edge and there it was, the Grand Canyon, the biggest, strongest thing you've ever seen. There was nowhere else to go, the earth ended and cracked in such a spectacular fashion that no human could traverse. I had read an article that summer that said they put a tracking collar on a mountain lion, and in a dead sprint it crossed the canyon without using a trail in just a few hours. The Park Rangers were shocked by the data. The mountain lion is sitting on a rock somewhere deep in the canyon right now, I mean right now, as you read this, the mountain lion is alive, living its mountain lion life. Can you see it?

To the east was the Navajo Reservation, the land was cracked, giant canyons carved in the land. To the west, the canyon went on endlessly, a limitless crack in the earth that had no intention of going anywhere.

I went in the tower, it had beautiful paintings and merchandise. I walked the old stairs to the top, and felt the walls, the walls that Mary Colter built. I imagined Mary Colter walking around, touching and examining every stone. Mary Colter knew one day she would die, every stone that made the tower was her life.

Back on the edge of the canyon, I was sitting by myself, Robin was looking at merchandise, Shufen was walking the edge, she had a giant smile on her face. I loved her smile. When she was close to the canyon, she felt joy, exhilaration, exuberance. There was something magical about her.

Out in the canyon, farther east, there was a place the Hopis called the Sipapu. It was where the first Hopis came into the world, into the Fourth World as they called it. They were in other worlds before, but one day, getting advice from a hummingbird they came through the Sipapu into our world. There are lots of legends about the Sipapu, some say two airplanes crashed into each other above the Sipapu, the planes crashed killing those inside, their bodies strewn over the earth. Some say if you sleep near the Sipapu, you may be sleeping in your tent, hear funny noises outside your tent, you rub your eyes, wake up your lover sleeping next to you, your lover says, "Why are you waking me up?" You say, "Do you hear that?" Your lover listens, and says, "Oh my god, what is that?" You both sit there scared, you both know you are hours of walking time from any other humans, from civilization, your cell phone doesn't work. There is no Wi-Fi at the Sipapu. You become scared, no one is used to hearing strange sounds in the middle of the night inside a tent. The mind imagines worse scenarios, axe murderers, rapists, violent criminals. But there are no violent criminals at the bottom of the canyon, there is nothing to steal but rocks and canyon views. One of you slowly unzips the tent door, you look around, and see groups of humans walking around, people who look like they could have been on the airplanes that crashed, some even look like Hopis from previous times, something is wrong with the people though, they aren't part of your world, they are there, but aren't there. Both you and your lover realize something weird is happening, some X-Files shit is going down, but you don't bother it. You watch it for a few minutes, and it slowly goes away, as if it was never there.

There were other legends, though, that white people had to stay away from it. The Sipapu was a hole in the canyon, and through this hole you could get to another reality. But the hole was not for white people, often when white people got within a mile of it, they became sick and would have to turn back, knowing their sickness would only heal if they went away. It is not discussed, but many white people had died going near the Sipapu, floods would come and wash them away, dehydration would strike them down, or they would fall, get injured and die an agonizing death inside the canyon. The Sipapu would not allow the white man to conquer this one last spot. The white man had taken everything, but there were spots in the Americas that could not be conquered, that would not budge.

The Bright Angel Bar

I was alone a lot, sitting in my room, thinking about her. Seriously I couldn't get her off my mind, sometimes I would think about her cat for hours. Her cat's name was Scipio, I asked her why she named her cat Scipio, she responded, "That's my favorite general." I laughed and said, "You have a favorite general?" She quickly responded, "Doesn't everyone?" She explained naked one night in bed — a January night in Ohio, snow covering every inch of the outside, snow covering the roads, snow covering the hoods of cars, snow covering the roofs, snow covering all the good earth. The heater turned on full blast, our bodies cuddled next to each other, gathering warmth with three mismatched comforters covering our bodies. She said her dad was into generals, he had a book on Scipio Africanus and thought it was a cool name. Scipio would crawl up on the bed and sleep next to us. It wasn't the best cat in the world, Scipio liked to fight with other cats, and make a lot of noise around 5:45 every morning, but he never crawled on our faces when we slept, which is pretty amazing for a cat.

I would think many dumb things about that cat, and her, but also her cat. I would eventually get tired of being in my room thinking stupid thoughts, and if I was thinking stupid thoughts, then stupid feelings would come. I didn't need all those bad feelings, but I couldn't stop them. I didn't want to feel or not feel the pain, it had to exist, the pain existed, I existed, I couldn't tell the pain to stop, it was me, and I was it, there was nowhere to go, I went to the Grand Canyon, I knew she would never follow me there. I knew she didn't care about hiking canyons, I don't want to say it, this is our secret, please don't tell anyone, but I knew. She didn't care about me anymore. She had moved on, she had plans, and they didn't involve me. Of course, I know, she didn't want bad things to happen to me, of course, she probably even thought I was still funny, but she didn't look at me and physically feel, "I want to hold him, I want to feel his naked body against mine." No, she didn't feel those things, when she was around me, she didn't feel any of those old feelings.

I got up from my bed, put on my pants and an okay looking wrinkled shirt and walked to the bar. There was pitch blackness, I had to stay alert, an elk could be anywhere, and boom, an elk horn gets stabbed into my chest. It was nice to worry about an elk killing me, I kept imagining an elk brutally murdering me, and felt a great sense of satisfaction in my demise.

I made it to the Bright Angel Hotel, then walked into the bar. The walls of the bar were covered in Hopi paintings of Natives doing random activities like dancing, in general hanging out, being people. I liked looking at the paintings.

The bartenders were a couple, they both worked out together all the time. The man was a big guy, about six-foot-six, big giant muscles, when he would come to the employee cafeteria he'd order two meals. He gave us speeches on how we could eat anything if we worked out an hour a day five days a week. He had lived in Germany for a short while, but I don't remember why, I think he said he married a German woman, or he was on a study abroad thing, but he also seemed like a liar.

His girlfriend was short, five-foot-two, but all muscle. She was always super excited and matter-of-fact. She ate a normal amount of food in the employee cafeteria.

The bartender couple had met at the canyon. They were both wandering the earth, they had no home and no truth, they found truth at the canyon. They had met three years earlier, he was a bartender and she was working in laundry. They met at the recreation center. Before they met each other, like all people, they felt alone, they felt like they would find no one they could truly love, they felt sad, they looked at other people with lovers and wedding rings and thought, "How did you get that ring? How did you find love? What did you do to deserve love in this hard world? What did I do not to deserve love?" They thought all those thoughts, they felt those thoughts deeply, but then they met each other in the gym at the recreation center, they kept seeing each other at the recreation center. They would say hi and talk for a few minutes. No one even remembers who asked who, some say it just happened, no different than the Colorado flowing through the canyon, they went to the cafeteria together, she ate one meal and he ate two. She liked how much he could eat in one sitting, she felt it was strong, he liked how she loved exercise, the sound of her laugh. They liked that they liked each other, because they felt at times that no one liked them, but there it was, right in front of them, somebody liking them. They weren't going to die alone, they weren't horrible, they weren't sinners, they were people that could be loved. And they would get the chance to love somebody else, they would get the chance to compromise and to take care of another living thing, to live alongside another human, a human just as terrified and weird as them. One day, one of them would die before the other one, they both knew, one would be left alone, but that was the deal, and like everyone else, they threw their chips down.

A short wiry guy was sitting by me, he was wearing a small cowboy hat. I had seen him around the park, he was a wrangler. He helped drive the mules down the canyon walls to Phantom Ranch at the bottom of the canyon, which was a little cabin/hotel that provided meals and a place to sleep for the hikers. Mules had to bring tourists and supplies down and the tourists and garbage back up. A few times while hiking the canyon trails I saw the wranglers and the mules. They were hot, sweat dripping down their faces, sweat dripping down the backs of the mules, a lot of sweat. They tried to use horses when the

111

canyon first opened up for tourists, but the horses didn't like the canyon cliffs and rugged trails.

I said to the man, "Aren't you a wrangler?"

He didn't look at me, he made it obvious he didn't care about me at all.

"Yeah, I'm a wrangler."

I said, "Well, where did you learn it?" I seriously had no idea how someone could become a wrangler, I was from Ohio, there were no wranglers in Ohio, I had a master's in creative writing, what the hell did I know about horses or the people who ride them?

The man still didn't look at me. "I learned in Kansas, my dad worked for a rancher, I had to help him work the animals since I was little," he said with a slight bitterness.

"You didn't like it?" I said. He seemed like the coolest person I had ever met. A cowboy, a real cowboy.

"No, I've spent my life working for ranchers, and all of them eventually won't want to pay you, or they tell you to get the hell out. We never sleep in nice places, I've never owned a house my whole life, I'm 35 and never got married. I don't got nothing to my name, I sleep on trails, I ride a mule in the hot sun. And these tourists don't know nothing, all day I gotta yell at them, I ain't having no fun out there."

I didn't know what to say, I didn't expect any of this. Cowboys are supposed to have wisdom, he had spent his life looking up at the stars, he had spent his life outside, with the trees and plains, standing on the prairie, an icon of American beauty and strength.

He didn't look at me, he went on, "I gotta wake up at 4am. tomorrow, I gotta get up, get dressed and get back on those mules. When winter comes, I gotta leave the park, they won't have enough work for me, I don't know where I'm going. I don't even know how to think about my future, there will be work somewhere, but with who, and will they pay me? What kind of bed will they give me to sleep on? Will I even have a pillow? I don't even have a car, I gotta travel by bus, maybe to Texas, maybe to Utah, who knows."

The wrangler finished his drink and left. He didn't seem happy that I spoke to him, that anyone alive spoke to him.

I ordered chicken wings.

A guy in his 40s came in, he was handsome, tall, perfectly-done hair, a firm, good body. He looked like the kind of man that saves women and children in movies. The kind of man that could kill people and make love to a model. Now, I've learned, that women who look like models are just women, they have their own specific tastes and desires. I've also learned that men who look like real men are just men and nothing to be worried about.

The man sat near me, he started talking to the bartenders about the trails. I decided to talk to him, I was lonely. I couldn't stop being lonely, the lonely had me, it wasn't something I could turn off. I was hoping a conversation with a handsome, powerful man would liberate me from the sad, creepy feeling of a wrangler traveling by bus across the length of Texas to find a hard bed to sleep on.

I told the man, there is a quiet trail called Hermit's Rest, there aren't many people out there, the only annoying thing was that helicopters flew over every half an hour.

The man looked annoyed by the Grand Canyon. He complained that the whole South Rim was overrun with tourists, it wasn't peaceful, it wasn't Alaska. He told all of us that he had taken a two-week trip to Alaska with his friend, that they hadn't seen another person for ten days, they were deep in the wild with no one around. He described the views, he described how awesome it was. We all listened.

Then he told us he was an arms contractor, that he did something with weapons, and it made him a lot of money. He said that his wife and kid were in the hotel room, that he finally got to sit by himself and enjoy a beer. He detailed his whole life, that he lived in Atlanta, he went to Georgetown University, he had been to Europe, Asia and even Ghana. I told him I went to Korea, he told me I should have gone to Harbin, China. He told us about his days in Harbin, he was doing a business deal there, the whole thing was paid for, the food was amazing.

I sat there listening, the bartenders stood there listening, our faces never changed, we never asked a question, the man kept talking. I was hoping the big guy would tell him to shut up, but the big guy knew the arms contractor was going to leave a big tip, the big man let him speak.

The man eventually left. Years later I hired a special investigator to find out if all the man's claims were true, the special investigator said that the man did go on a trip to Alaska but it was a specially built trip for wealthy tourists. They were put on a trail, with their rented gear, they had GPS and walkie-talkies, and helicopters were ready at all times in case of rescue. Yes, the man went to Harbin, but the man hated the food, the man had diarrhea the entire time, and as he pooped he scorned the entire cultural history of China.

I ate my chicken wings. Ordered another beer.

The night could not end, I ordered a shot. What could it matter? Maybe if I jumped off the edge of the canyon, walked into it, never came back. There was a story, years ago, a park ranger was hiking off trail and found a skeleton, a human skeleton. A human had walked down the trail, most likely with the intention of suicide. They had walked off the trail deeper and deeper into the canyon, sat down next to a tree, and let dehydration kill them. On a hot summer day the sun can kill you in hours. But maybe the skeleton got lost, maybe the skeleton became disoriented, was thinking deeply about something, perhaps Aristotle or South American dictatorships, maybe a hummingbird told the skeleton that the truth wasn't on the trail. The skeleton kept walking and walking, getting more and more lost, until there was no return. The skeleton laid down in the canyon, let go, and was taken by death.

Maybe I could do that? Go into the canyon, get lost and let go, let death take me. But I knew I wouldn't do that, I enjoyed missing her too much. I indulged in my misery, there was no intention of ending it. The cowboy was the same as me, but I was better at hiding it. The arms contractor didn't feel miserable at all, he was too busy trying to make sure no one thought he was a loser. I didn't care if people thought I was a loser, because I didn't think of any of them as losers. I wasn't a winner either, I wasn't good or evil, I wasn't beyond or below, I was a bunch of horizontals. If I was a superhero, I would be called Horizontal Man. I wasn't average either, I couldn't be horizontal, I was I was I was, I ordered another shot, I had tried so hard all my life, I put so much pressure on myself to be an amazing person, an interesting person, I was that arms contractor, a man who needs other people to look at him fondly, I had a master's, I had traveled the world, and I loved mentioning it. The need to be impressive, the need to be the coolest guy in the room, to be smart, to know things other people didn't know, for example, the capital of Azerbaijan is Baku. I can write and speak a little Korean, I learned one time Marcel Proust met James Joyce and one asked the other, "Do you like truffles?" Why did I learn all these things, why did I show up to class on time and get good grades, why did I study so hard for the GRE, why did I go to Korea, why did I take the bus in cold ass winter Korea so many times, just so she could leave me? I tried, I tried and tried, and the universe did not give me what I wanted. I thought, I knew, yes, I knew it, that if we do what is right, if we work hard, if we behave, the results should be in our favor, but they weren't, and I couldn't even remember what exactly happened. I looked around the bar, she wasn't there. I was not in Korea, there were no Buddhist temples, no cell phone stores blaring K-pop, no kimbap shops, no taxis, no scooters, no old Korean women cutting vegetables on the sidewalk. I was no longer a teacher, I was a cashier, Korea was gone, my job was gone, she was gone, there was nothing but me, sitting in a bar on the edge of the Grand Canyon.

After Billy Cox left the bar, the big guy said to his girlfriend, "I think something bad happened to Billy."

She responded while wiping the counter, "But he doesn't want to talk about it, he would probably feel better if he talked about it."

"And it is like, I think he asks all those questions to other people so he never has to talk about himself." the big guy said.

"Oh, yeah, to avoid his own life, he just listens to other people, he wants to think about other people, not himself."

The big guy said, "I hope he feels better one day, but it won't be soon."

The Senegalese and Jamaicans

The Grand Canyon had a lot of foreign workers, but mostly from Asia and Eastern Europe, a few from Latin America. There were no Africans.

I was working cashier at the employee cafeteria, five of the most beautiful, healthy-looking people walked in, I remember smiling. They looked confused, they walked up to the counter, but like, bumping into each other and other people. It sounded like they were all speaking French, but I don't know French, so I didn't know exactly.

Everyone in line was looking around at what was going on, trying to figure out what they should be doing. I remembered in Korea how the older people had no comprehension of lines, everyone stood around and eventually took their turns. Remembered getting bumped hard by an old woman in Korea once.

I stood up and waved at them, "Hey guys, we have to stand in lines."

They looked at me, their facial expressions were immensely perplexed. The same thing happened to them that happened to all the foreign students working at the Grand Canyon, they were in college, someone came to their college and offered them a chance to work in America and get paid. They had to get a passport, fill out forms and pay for a work visa. They told all their family and friends that they were going to America, that their dream was coming true. They were going to have an experience they would never forget. But they didn't realize they would actually be in another country, with completely different customs, completely different modes of behavior.

Before people go abroad, they base everything off movies they have seen, they imagine all kinds of scenarios that will never happen. They know nothing, and they don't know it.

The young people were from Senegal (and to be honest, I know nothing of Senegal, I had at that moment in my life no knowledge of Senegal, all I knew was that the capital is Dakar, they speak French and it is on the west coast of Africa. Three years have passed, and those are still the only facts I know about Senegal.) Less than three days ago they got on a plane in Dakar, all five of them super excited, laughing, making jokes, boasting about what they would do in America, boundless energy and hope. None of them had ever been on a long plane ride, the first thing they had to do was be on a plane for ten hours, then they had a layover probably in New York or Atlanta. Hours spent in a chrome-looking airport with expensive food to eat. Hours and hours passed, some of them started to feel frustrated with the existence of time itself, they finally arrive in Flagstaff, still 90 miles by car to go. As they are being driven up 180 to the Grand Canyon they see open spaces with nothing in it, just endless nothing. They started to think, "What the hell have I done? This isn't like American movies, this isn't American television, this is some wild world where humans don't live."

I started motioning with my hands for the Senegalese to come get in line, they weren't really responding. Then a woman, with a beautiful face, a face like I've never seen before, said, "We stand in line?" in a thick accent.

I didn't respond verbally, I just motioned, smiled, and hoped they got what I was saying.

They made it to the front of the line, they stood before the American food, looking at it, they kept talking to each other in French, they were all confused. It was burrito day, but they had never seen a burrito in their entire lives.

Then the woman said, "Pig? No pig."

The cook and I stared at them, "No pig?"

Then they said, "We are Muslim."

The cook looked at me, he didn't know what the hell was going on. The cook spent his nights in a drunken stupor watching movies from the recreational center DVD library, he had never cared about Christianity let alone Islam.

"Okay," I said. I went over to the cook area and pointed at the meat one by one, I pointed at bacon and said, "Pig." Then pointed at white chunks of meat and said, "Chicken, you know chicken." After I said anything they would talk for almost a minute, discussing the possible meanings and implications of every word. Then I pointed at ground taco beef and said, "Cow." Then they talked more. After much conversation they decided on chicken tacos. They sat down together holding their chicken tacos, we watched them put the chicken tacos in their mouths and begin to chew, they liked it.

Every time they came in we had to notify them of what was pork and not pork. The old white woman who ran cashier in the morning didn't like it, she didn't like having to point out the different meats, but she did it anyway.

The Senegalese were always confused. As time passed I learned the beautiful woman's name was Odette. She would often come to me on behalf of everyone and ask me questions, I would go and help her and we would try together to solve their problems.

The only other black foreigners were the Jamaicans, but they were different. They were from the New World, they understood North American ways better than any of the Europeans or Asians.

The Jamaicans would spend their extra time sitting at the recreational center watching television, they really liked *Martin*. There was a channel that played several episodes of *Martin* in a row, they would sit quietly and watch the shows. The Jamaicans never really drank, I never saw a drunk Jamaican, nor did I ever see a drunk Senegalese. But they all had headphones on with music playing all the time, there was one Jamaican in my dorm that needed music so badly, that he would bring speakers with him to the shower, he would play reggaeton while he showered.

One day I was standing on the second-floor staircase, looking out at the elk walking down the train tracks, in between the ponderosa pines. The Senegalese were walking and a group of Jamaicans were walking, they had never met. As they walked up to each other, one young Senegalese man and one young Jamaican man reached their fists out, they bumped their fists, after 400 years of separation, they had found each other again. The Jamaicans looked into their faces and they could see themselves. They could see their mothers, their fathers, their brothers, their cousins, they could see that their faces and bodies came from somewhere. They would probably never go, but they knew, somewhere on this earth, there was a whole country of people that looked like them. The Senegalese looked at them, they knew, they were the stolen mother, the stolen father, the stolen brother, the stolen sister, the stolen cousin, that these people had known great suffering in the New World.

But it was like it wasn't that long ago at all, time had brought them back together, the canyon had brought them back together. They began to talk and laugh, eventually they began to hang out and have little parties where they would dance together. The river of the Colorado flows and flows.

Perseids with Christians

When I was working cashier in the employee cafeteria, more than half of the summer was over, but right before the Perseids something really bad happened. I went to the library where we could use the Wi-Fi. The foreign workers would all sit at picnic tables outside talking to their family members on Skype. At any given time of the day, you might see Romanians, Taiwanese or Filipinos on Skype, waving at their mothers and fathers, telling them they were having a good time, maybe complaining a little. Everyone pretending for their parents' sake that they were okay and that they were safe, that they weren't spending their nights fighting off raccoons or drinking themselves into a stupor.

I didn't expect anything when I went to the library, I was having a normal day. The day was normal, I was normal, the elk looked normal. I turned on my computer at a picnic table, she was online, I asked her if she wanted to talk on Skype, she said yes. I still felt at that moment, right before the Skype started, hope. I had hope that she would say, "Please come back, I made a mistake, I can't imagine my life without you, when I think about my future, I want you to be next to me. I want you to hold my hand for a thousand years, I want to cuddle you on the sofa, I want your kisses. When I think about getting married, I think about getting married to you. When I think about having babies, they are your babies. I can see it in my mind, we live in a nice house, we both have great jobs we enjoy, we come home from work, and there you are, standing in the kitchen, a man, my man. I can see you playing in the yard with our daughter or son, I can see you helping our kids with their homework. I can even see you putting up the Christmas tree."

Every time I had a free moment, I would imagine her saying that to me, right up till that moment.

When I went on Skype she was in her new bedroom, in her new apartment. She smiled at me, there she was, the woman I had loved for so long. She was on the screen, she was speaking to me, she was paying attention to me. But then she said things, sad things, things that I did not want to hear, what she was saying hurt so much. I couldn't take it, it felt like a raccoon had crawled into my chest and was trying to violently kill me from the inside. I felt like I was experiencing a stroke, a heart attack, a seizure and several gun shots at once. All of reality started cracking, going blurry, sounds, the earth, there are no words, it was painful, very painful.

I closed the computer. Started walking back to Victor Annex. My mind started racing at a thousand miles an instant, I couldn't stop it, my chest was screaming, too much scattered energy inside me, I couldn't control it. I had to call her, I had to ask again if it was true, if she was sure, I pressed the button, she picked up, she cared about me, but she did not love me. I was walking by the mule barn, the mules cared nothing about my troubles. I started saying while crying, "I have lost, I have lost, I never lose, I had you, I had you, but I lost, I lost," then I had a panic attack, crying hysterically in front of the mules, hyperventilating. I laid down by the mule barn, I couldn't move, it all went black, a total fugue state. The mules saw a grown man in his 30s lying by the road crying and hyperventilating. The mules came over and looked at me. I couldn't move, I couldn't get my mind back. I think I went somewhere, I couldn't physically handle what was happening, my mind had to go black to deal with the present.

The next thing I remember is Dream walking me back to Victor Annex, he was having me drink water, Dream kept saying, "Billy you okay, Billy you okay?" I couldn't respond, I couldn't get my thoughts to settle on one voice, a cacophony of voices was screaming at once, I had many minds, and no single mind could take control. Dream's strong arm was holding me up, my feet felt weak, like I was floating. He got me up to my room and laid me down. I sat in the bed staring at the ceiling, I hadn't felt so terrified, so incapable, since I was a teenager trapped in my parents' house, trapped in that small town in Ohio. I was a man, I wasn't supposed to cry, but something broke in me. Dream sat on the edge of the bed, he held my hand and I said, "I lost, Dream, my heart, my heart hurts." Dream looked down at me and said, "She wasn't the one, you will live a long life, someone else will come, it won't be tomorrow, but they will come."

Dream left me, I went to sleep and did not wake for twelve hours.

I was standing behind the register, Chandra and Nate came in wearing their housing uniforms. They always came in after work and had a bite to eat together. I became closer friends with Nate, we would often sit at night with Pin-Yu from Taiwan and play the guitar together. We would trade the guitar back and forth, I would play 90s rock, Nate would play more recent music and Pin-Yu would play Chinese pop songs. Nate and Pin-Yu would play with their fingers, but I played with a pick.

While Chandra and Nate paid for their food, they asked me if I wanted to watch the Perseids with them and the other kids from the Christian group. I felt a little apprehensive, I never did anything with the Christians, beside attend the church service on the edge sometimes. Since the mule barn incident I'd begun drinking heavily at night. I would sit on a log, with friends, listen to sad music on a little speaker, eat buffalo wings, fight off raccoons, and complain about my life. I said, "Yes." Chandra and Nate seemed sincere when they asked me, I could never say no to sincerity.

I met them in front of Maswik a few hours later, everyone seemed really excited. I got in the backseat of a car with two other

125

people, everyone was talking about their lives, when their last day at the canyon was, when they had to start school. I stayed quiet, I didn't want to talk about myself.

We went down to the West Rim. During the day cars weren't allowed on that part of the road because of the tour buses, but after the sunset, cars could drive down. It was pitch black down that road. Chandra, who was driving, said, "Oh my gosh, I have never driven such a dark road in my life." Everyone was slightly paranoid that we would hit an elk or deer.

We arrived at Hopi Point, there was no one there, we had the whole canyon to ourselves, the silence, we could hear the river rushing deep in the canyon.

There were eight of us, we all lay down on the cold rock. Everyone was lying down on their backs staring straight up except for Sabrina, I didn't know anything about Sabrina, she had red hair and was short. She had a beautiful guitar she put on her knee, as we all laid there looking up at the meteors shoot through the darkness. Sabrina sang songs about several of her friends there, we all sat quietly listening to the songs, they were funny songs, we all laughed. After each song was over Sabrina talked about why she wrote it the way she did, everyone commented and she sang another song. Then after the personal songs were over, she began to sing Christian songs, everyone began singing. Seven voices singing out at Hopi Point in the pitch-black night. Every time a meteor was witnessed a "wow" and a "woo" was said. It was beautiful to hear them sing that night.

Sheila

I didn't know anything, and I knew it. There was a moment in Korea, I was walking down the street on a humid summer night, half-drunk with my friend David. We saw a drunk Korean man wearing a suit sleeping on the street, curled up in a little ball, vomit all over him. I looked at David and said, "Dave, I don't know anything." David responded, "There isn't anything to know."

For years I lived in Ohio, there were no Native Americans in Ohio. In Ohio there were white people, Italian people and African-Americans. There were trees, there were ponds, a few lakes, all the lakes had been made by the ideas and hands of men and women. Culture in Ohio, was it even real? Men would mow the grass, the grass had to be mowed. The leaves fell in the fall, the men would rake the leaves and put them in piles in the backyard. Everyone had basements, some basements were made into extra living rooms, as in, rooms where people lived, watched television and played video games.

In Ohio, men and women went to factories, they went to steel mills, they went to foundries. They wore blue jeans, listened to classic rock and went to work. The mother and father in the living room watching television, the children going to soccer and baseball practice. The church having a Veteran's Day pancake breakfast for a local person in need of help. Friday night high school football games, everyone supported the local team, sixty-year-old men that didn't have sons on the team would go, watching the young men hustle and try to win on the field. The marching bands, majorettes, the cheerleaders, moms and dads running the concessions, drinking hot chocolate from Styrofoam cups. Mrs. Anderson selling raffle tickets, Mr. Kranes announcing the game, and Mrs. Baker drunk again, she slipped in mud and fell over. A few junior high kids laughed, but everyone felt sorry for her son Chuck.

There was no spirituality, they didn't dance in the street like Pungmol dancers, there were no Buddhist temples in the forest, they didn't have ornate buildings to their Gods, a long history of great minds and generals to look back on for inspiration. There were men with lawnmowers, there were plastic lawn chairs, drag race cars in the garages, televisions, Snickers and Butterfingers, Wal-Mart was the biggest building in town. I couldn't find a dream there, I couldn't, I wanted to stand in front of that town and say, "I'm sorry, but I couldn't find my dream here, I don't hate any of you. I know now, people don't usually leave their home, most Koreans never move away from Korea, most Filipinos stay in the Philippines. Most people stay where they are born, but you know, if you want to stay where you're born, you have to own it, you have to make it your dream. You have to find the Gods that live in your area, you have to find the songs that the trees and birds sing, you have to build temples, you have to write poems for your people. You have to grow food, you have to dream, because you are the history of this place, I don't know where my home is, I have not gotten there yet, it is out there, somewhere in my future, it exists, time will locate me somewhere, but I cannot stay here."

There were no Native Americans in Ohio.

I was working the register in the employee cafeteria, Sheila was there that day. She was sitting with her friend Rosa. Rosa was a big Navajo woman in her 40s. Rosa had lived in the park for five years. She had no boyfriend or kids. She was kind of weird, she always wore a fanny pack and would get anxiety when we were out of things she wanted to eat.

I had recently bought a Native American-style belt from the Hopi House, I really liked it. It had beautiful colors and a shiny belt buckle. It made me feel Western, like I was a little cowboy when I was wearing it. I wanted to feel something those days, I wanted to feel proud and strong, but good feelings wouldn't come, there was sadness, sometimes it would grow into feelings of frustration and bitterness. I kept yelling at people, a few days before I'd yelled at a learning-disabled cook over rice. A musician playing in the bar ordered rice, but the musician specified that the rice be put in tiny to-go containers not on a plate. The musician told me it verbally, he didn't tell the cook. When the cook was about to finish the order I said, "Hey, could you throw the rice in containers."

The cook was like, "No, they aren't supposed to go in containers."

"The guy asked for it, it is okay."

The learning-disabled cook said sternly, "He didn't ask me."

I still felt calm and said, "But he asked me, it is okay."

The guy responded, "But he didn't ask me, that's not where rice goes."

Then a flood of emotion, bad emotion, not good emotion, totally bleak creepy vicious emotion, surged through me, I hit the counter with a fist and yelled, "Put the rice in the container, what is the big deal!!!"

There I was, a man with a master's degree yelling at a guy who had dropped out of ninth grade, never had a driver's license and had no hope of ever, for the rest of his life on this planet, getting a nice office job, making $50,000 a year with a 401k plan. I knew, and everyone else knew, I would one day get a normal job and marry a moderately attractive woman with a spunky personality. I would probably even have a kid in the future, and that kid would even love me. But that cook, he was screwed, he would never make more than $17,000 a year, he was never going to get married or have kids or live a decent life. He had at least 30 to 50 more years to live, and was going to do all of it alone. He was going to wake up every day for the rest of his life knowing it was psychologically impossible for him to transcend his limitations, and there I was, yelling at his agony.

I didn't have it together.

Sheila and her friend Rosa were sitting at a table, Sheila was rolling silverware. Sheila rolled silverware for hours, as she sat there older Navajos would come and visit her. One was an old dishwasher named Steve, he always wore a baseball cap, his skin wrinkled and worn. He always called everyone "boss." But he pronounced it in a funny way, you would walk by him and he would be holding a broom and he would say peacefully, "Bawssssssss." I never asked him why he did it, but he always did it, and eventually I started saying it back to him.

I walked over wearing my new Native American belt, Sheila liked it, but Rosa made fun of me, she told me I should get a pair of moccasins too. I smiled, they asked me where the belt was made, I told them, "In China." Everyone laughed. We talked about how the best belts and Native jewelry were in Santa Fe. I told them I had been in The Plaza in Santa Fe. Rosa said she passed through in '98 and Sheila had been there a few times to visit a cousin. Everyone loved Santa Fe. We agreed they had the best sunsets in America

After Rosa finished her meal, she left. She never really said goodbye, she would just get up and leave.

I told Sheila how I read the Diné Bahane'. She was impressed, but told me, that they were always written by the bilagáana. That's what she would call me and all white people, "bilagáana." In Korea they called me waeguk, in Arizona I became a bilagáana. At least I was something. In Ohio, I wasn't anything but "that guy."

Then Sheila taught me some Navajo words, she seemed excited to be the teacher, and I wanted her to teach me. Before, I had been the language teacher. I wanted someone else to play the role for a minute, because I knew I would be teaching English again soon enough.

She wrote on yellow notepad paper, the word for good morning: "Yá'át'ééh abiní."

She had me pronounce it slowly, we practiced together, she smiled.

Then she wrote down the word for goodbye: "Hágoónee." We practiced saying it together, I smiled, she smiled, things felt right for a second. When the Navajo security guard came in, she had me say, "Yá'át'ééh abiní." The man laughed, and told a story about when he met a bilagáana that knew Navajo perfectly.

I took the notes Sheila made for me, put them in my pocket, and kept them for years.

Sheila had a story though, people would tell her to date again, a lot of the men at the canyon thought she was a wonderful woman. Sheila always responded, "Never again!" She told me she was once married to a bilagáana from Ohio, a long, long time ago. She never specified when, it could have been 40 years ago, she said the man beat her good. She said one time she came home from working all day and found him cheating in her house, and instead of him saying he was sorry, he beat her instantly for catching him.

"Never again!"

Lying on the Forest Floor

A few weeks earlier, Kaja Marcelina and I hiked down to the bottom of the canyon. We woke up early, met at Maswik, ate a big breakfast. I kept telling them, "Eat as much as you can." We all ate sausage, cheese, bacon and eggs rolled in tortilla shells. We weren't tired, we were excited. They were 22 years old and full of exuberance and youthful power. There is nothing in the universe as full of energy as a 22-year-old, armies have known this for thousands of years. The old leaders and generals ask, "What do we do? The enemy is coming." Someone responds, "Send a bunch of 22-year-olds at them."

I was happy to be hiking with such energetic people.

During the whole hike, Marcelina led, she knew where she was going. Both of the young women were gym rats in their home country, and according to them women lifted weights, they didn't just do cardio and yoga like they do in America. They didn't care if boys thought they looked strong and muscular, they had their own goals, their own ideals and imaginations to take care of, a man could deal with it or he couldn't, not their problem.

During the hike Kaja made a million mule poop jokes. Marcelina stayed relatively quiet but couldn't stop laughing and smiling.

When we reached the bottom, we sat at a picnic table eating lunch. Kaja and Marcelina pulled out Snickers bars, those small ones bought in a ten pack. I told them to buy Clif Bars, I told them chocolate would melt, but they bought what they wanted. They opened the packages, it was brown goo, they sat there licking the brownness of the candy wrappers, I couldn't stop laughing.

133

We all sat in the creek together, the cool water of the Colorado flowed around us. We needed it, it woke us up, returned us to lively feelings. We marched back up the canyon walls. Usually the higher I got, the slower I moved. But Marcelina wouldn't let that happen, Marcelina was muscle and health and vitality, she wanted to get up the canyon walls.

On our way up we saw these strangely dressed people, a woman and a man both wearing bikinis and giant black sunglasses. We asked them where they were from, they said, "Brooklyn." Hipsters at the bottom of the canyon.

When we were walking through Indian Gardens, we saw a German dad and son, I asked them how they were doing, if they had hiked the canyon before. The man said he had hiked the canyon when he was 21 in 1980 and knew he had to bring his son to hike it.

When we got to the top the sun was setting, we had done it. We had made it to the bottom and back to the top together, which was like sharing blood. Hiking the canyon leaves a deep imprint on your mind, on your soul, maybe even your eternal soul, that even in Heaven, in future lives, you are always connected to those people you've been to the bottom of the canyon with.

A few days after we went to the bottom, the fog and rain started. Rains came down, the creeks flooded, buildings flooded, rain poured down on us. I would sit in the employee cafeteria and watch the clouds cast shadows, then rain would come down hard. Every time it rained in the employee cafeteria we would have to get a big garbage can, because the roof leaked horribly by the entrance.

Then a fog came, I had never seen anything like it, I was from Ohio, I had seen some good fogs. But this fog engulfed everything. The canyon would fill full of fog, or cloud, it was white like cotton and couldn't be seen through. Tourists would show up with dreams of seeing the canyon and instead of there being amazing colors, with endless beauty in all directions, they saw nothing but a giant unbelievable cloud that had ruined their vacation.

When the cloud would move out from the canyon, it came up like a wave of white smoke, there was no visibility. There you were, in the desert, surrounded by Utah Junipers, Ponderosa Pines, and rattlesnakes, and instead of a dryness, an unbearable heat, you found yourself surrounded by a white fog. After the first two days it was interesting, on the third day, fog depression sank in. I started to lose my mind in that fog, other people did too, the world made no sense, it was like a horror movie.

One day the fog went away and we had a few days of reprieve from the dangerous sadness that was infecting all of us. Kaja asked me to spend the night with her, I didn't push anything with Kaja. I needed, at that moment in my life, friends/companions more than I needed a lover. Being friendly with Kaja was good, it was simple, we both needed friends at that moment. (Kaja might not agree with this, she might have thought we were in love, that I was going to go to Poland, get married and be happy.)

Kaja and I walked around the South Rim on a star-filled night. We held hands, her hand felt soft in mine. The first thing we did was go to the seating area where people waited for the Hermit's Rest bus. A violent wind came out of the canyon, there was no wind at the top of the canyon, it came from the inside. We sat and let the wind hit us, sitting close with our bodies touching. She told me about Madrid, and how she went to Valencia and played on the beach all day. Kaja loved the beach, she loved running around mostly naked, drinking a few alcoholic beverages and swimming in the salty water. She showed me pictures from her Facebook page of her Madrid days, she excitedly told me about each friend and location.

Kaja said she had dated a man there, a native of Spain. She loved her Spaniard, he was handsome and could dance well. She even gave him her virginity, she said she trusted him, but he lied. I asked what he lied about, she responded sadly, "He had another girl." I sat there thinking, "I don't have another girl, but I feel like I'm lying." She talked about him for a long time, as the wind hit us. It was like she was throwing these dark thoughts over the cliff of the canyon, every painful feeling she spoke, she would walk over to the edge and say, "This is my pain canyon, here is what he did to me, here is what I felt in my dorm room, crying alone in Spain. Here, take it, my pain." And the canyon responded, "I will take your pain Kaja." Somebody had hurt Kaja, somebody had hurt me, somebody had hurt Sheila. We were the kind of people that got hurt, we didn't like it, but we were sensitive, and we wanted to please our lovers, we wanted to make them happy, and their happiness often meant hurting us.

Kaja and I walked away from the edge, we walked down the little streets which led to the Maswik laundry building. It was a secluded area in the forest. The ground was dry, Kaja told me to lie down on the forest floor, I couldn't ever remember doing that, even in Ohio. But the soil was always moist in Ohio, just like in Poland. In Arizona the soil was dry, even if it had rained a few hours before. I laid down on the ground, then she put her little body on top of me, she just kind of hung out on top of me, wiggling around and talking. I told her I had a friend who always said, "I wish I was a strong black man who was an awesome rapper, I wish I was a Hispanic guy who played baseball, I wish I had the attitude of Freddie Mercury, I wish I had the looks of Ryan Gosling, if I was a woman I would want to be Stevie Nicks. He had all these weird things he wanted to be, but the one thing he never wanted to be was himself, he never desired to wake up and be himself, he didn't want to experience life as himself." I told Kaja I wanted to be a legend, I wanted people to remember me, because I would impact their life in some way, it didn't matter if it was a cashier at Starbucks, a student I was teaching, or if I wrote a book and people really liked it. It didn't matter to me who it was, because everyone deserved to encounter one friendly person every day of their lives. Kaja liked that, she said it was hard sometimes to be friendly with men because she was young and pretty, but she always tried to be kind. She went on and told me she wanted to be a legend too, that she couldn't just live in Poznan. She said, there were people who never left Poznan, and she didn't want to be one of them. She wanted to travel, she wanted to experience things and learn from this world. That life was not a joke to her, it was something to be taken seriously. That she was going to go back to Poznan and get a master's in business and work for a company and make a lot of money, and keep traveling the world, and maybe someday end up back in America or Spain, her true loves.

Kaja was young, naturally she still had naivety and innocence, but just like the young Taiwanese women, the young Filipino women, the young Jamaican women, and the young Navajo women, the future of her culture was inside them. These young women had dreams, they had imaginations, powerful convictions that would not stop them. In 2035 they would be the leaders of companies, doctors and politicians. And all of them loved Beyoncé, the Romanians, the Jamaicans, even the Taiwanese, they knew Beyoncé, it was like an African Eve had emerged from the agony of 3,000 years of patriarchal civilization and said, "Don't be afraid, not anymore, we are the future." In eras before, the heroes were Generals, Kings, men of industry, but now, the heroes were women musicians, writers and politicians. The canyon changed slowly, but in the civilizations of the world, there was a revolution taking place, but women did not fight with bombs and murder, with prisons and executions. Women would win this war by waking up earlier than men, putting their makeup on, doing their hair, showing up to work and doing a damn good job for years on end. Men had momentary bursts of brute strength, but women contained decades of toughness that men could not compete with.

We spent several hours lying on the forest floor. Her body on top of me felt so perfect. But I couldn't stop time, because if time stopped that night, I would have felt fine with it, time did not stop, we had to get up and walk back to her cabin. When we made it back to her room, we got in our underwear and went under the covers together. We cuddled up tight and went to sleep.

New Hance Trail

When we got the permit to hike New Hance Trail, the National Park Ranger told Shufen and I, "It is the hardest trail on the South Rim, this is a serious trail, there is no water, no one will be down there to help you if something goes wrong. No one has got a permit for that trail in three weeks, no one will be there"

Shufen looked at me, shrugged, said, "We do it," then she smiled.

I said, "Yes, we do it."

A friend dropped us off a little past Moran Point. There was no sign along the road for New Hance Trail, the National Park Rangers didn't want tourists to hike it, thinking it would be an easy trail.

We walked into the forest, looking around for the trail. It took a few minutes, but Shufen spotted it, she yelled, "Billy, here."

The sign was there, New Hance Trail.

New Hance wasn't a trail, it was just a way down that might not kill you. No one ever went on it, it wasn't maintained, in 20 years it would probably be forgotten, and in a way it was already forgotten.

We started our way down the canyon walls. It was weird hiking with Shufen, she didn't know English very well, I couldn't make jokes, I couldn't utilize my sense of sarcasm and irony to make her laugh, I couldn't tell long stories about my life in other countries. Which made me think at times, why does she like me? Those are my best qualities. Kaja loves those qualities in me. But why do I like her? I looked at her walking ahead of me, I too, could barely understand anything she said, but we had the trail in common, we had the canyon. We needed something the other had to give, but it was not obvious, it was too deep, it was a spiritual understanding. There was a part of me that believed I had met her before, in some other life, maybe not a past life, maybe in a future life we both had yet to live. I imagined a monk accompanying a nun in 7th Century China or 11th Century Italy, the Master or Priest told us we had to travel together, we walked for a few days discussing the Good Word, said our goodbyes and never sew each other again.

As we were hiking down, a condo of California condors floated in the sky. There were at least ten of them, swirling in circles, never flapping their wings, it was silent and beautiful. Shufen pointed and said, "Condor." I said, "Yes, condor." She said, "Beautiful." I smiled.

We kept walking while the California condors floated in the canyon.

The first section resembled a forest, a lot of trees and green, but soon it disappeared, then the rocks came. There were no markings anywhere, no signs pointing in any direction, randomly there would be cairns, but Shufen didn't understand cairns, she called them "rockies." So I called them rockies too.

The way down was steep. It felt at times like we were going straight down, like we were falling. Eventually we got to this huge boulder. It looked like we couldn't pass. We could do nothing but scramble, we had to really climb those rocks, it felt good to use my hands, to hold the rocks and tree limbs, to pull myself up. After one huge obstacle, Shufen stood up on the rock and said, "I am Spiderwoman," and smiled. I remembered the vision of the Hopis, how a Spider Grandma lived in the desert, was Shufen Spider Grandma, had I found myself with a mystic spirit?

We walked farther down the path, we found water, a little four-inch-wide, eight-inch-deep creek going through the rock. We were happy, we pulled the water filter and sucked up water, filtered it, and put the creek water in our bottles. We knew there wasn't much water on the trail, we had to stay focused on always having water, without water, we would die.

After three hours we entered the wash, the sun was strong, it was around 95 degrees at the bottom of the canyon, we were hot and the sun would not relent. We sat on a rock and ate peanut butter sandwiches, we felt dazed, the world seemed blurry. A hummingbird flew to us, the hummingbird hovered less than two feet in front of us, moving around in the air, darting back and forth. I looked at Shufen, she was looking directly at the hummingbird, she was smiling. I smiled too. After a few minutes the bird zipped away.

We hiked in the heat, we arrived at a steep part that made no sense. We had no idea where we had to go, there were no rockies anywhere, Shufen looked and said, "No rockies." We started to get worried, where were we? Had the trail disappeared in an avalanche of rocks, would we have to turn back? I went down below, walking on red rock, she went above. She found the path, but I was down below, there was fifteen feet of cliff to scramble, I threw my bag up to her, she held it, I grabbed the rocks, slowly putting my feet in good places, and pulled myself up. Shufen grabbed me and helped me get the last inches. I had total trust in Shufen, she would not let me die in the canyon.

We walked to where she thought we should go, and there was nothing, we walked back to where we started, and then noticed we had gone right instead of left, the path was there the whole time. We laughed, we saw rockies, and kept walking.

We made it to the river, there it was the Colorado River, the unusable river that had disappointed the conquistadors and industrialists. The Colorado River stands at war with industrial civilization, boats can't go down it, to get to the river bank one has to trek over rocks and lands empty of green and water. I loved it. I loved it because it could not be tamed.

There was a sandy/muddy beach we stood on, the water was brown like milk chocolate. Shufen and I couldn't stop smiling. We found the campground close by, there were these little rocks put in what looked like an intentional order, Shufen said, "This place is old, many years ago, people like Navajos lived here."

We put our bags down and went back to the beach. As I was standing there looking at the water, Shufen yelled, "Billy, help, help." I turned around and Shufen was breast deep in mud. I stared at her for a second and thought, "Is she in quicksand?" Then it hit me, "Oh my god, Shufen is in quicksand!" I ran over, Shufen put her hands on my arms and I pulled her out. Shufen was covered in mud. "Oh my god Shufen, you are covered in mud."

Shufen laughed and said, "Yes, muddy." We laughed.

Shufen didn't care about her mud problem, she pulled the legs of her pants up, took off her shoes and walked in the river. The water was ice cold, but Shufen didn't care.

I sat on the muddy beach and watched the brown water rushing, while Shufen kept making noises while playing with branches in the water. Her enthusiasm was unbelievable, I had never seen a human so one with nature.

After the sun went down, we had to gather water from the brown river, we had to put it in a bag and let the silt go to the bottom of the bag before we could filter it to make it drinkable. Shufen and I walked to the river in the darkness, it was real darkness. There was no electricity, no illumination, the light was silent as the sounds. We were alone, no one would be able to reach us for six hours by foot, our cell phones didn't work, not even helicopters could save us. It was the most alone we had ever been in our entire lives, the most dangerous.

As we were walking down the little path to the river, Shufen stopped to look at something, I walked ahead, then suddenly I fell into the quicksand. I was chest deep in the mud. I turned, expecting Shufen to be right behind me, but she wasn't. Then I heard her yell, "Billy! Billy! Look," then something I didn't understand. I yelled back, "Shufen, help me! I'm in quicksand!" But then I remembered she wasn't going to understand anything I said. She probably assumed I was yelling back, "Sounds awesome." I doubt Shufen knew the word "quicksand," as I sank into the mud I thought about if I ever taught my students in Korea the word "quicksand." Definitely not, I thought. I realized after a minute that Shufen was not going to stop playing around and help me. I pulled myself out of the mud angrily, I crawled over away from the mud, then I realized I didn't have one of my shoes on, oh god no! I couldn't walk up the canyon without a shoe, that would be a real horror story. I had to get the shoe out before the hole where my leg was closed over with wet mud. I crawled back over, stuck my body into the mud face first, reached in with my hand, sticking my arm deep in the quicksand. My hand found the shoe, I clenched it, and pulled my body out. My face and hair were covered in my mud, my clothes were totally covered. My shoes were completely caked.

I stood up, I don't know how much time passed, it felt like ten minutes, but it was probably only 45 seconds.

I ran down the path to Shufen, I yelled, "Shufen, I fell in the quicksand!"

She was standing there, peaceful, she pointed at something on the ground. I looked over and there was a pink rattlesnake. I stood there looking at it, it was beautiful. My heart felt perfect looking at that pink rattlesnake. I said smiling, "It's a rattlesnake Shufen." She took pictures with her cell phone and said, "Beautiful." We were less than three feet away, it was so close, I felt no fear, only happiness, the pink rattlesnake seemed like our friend, the hummingbird seemed like our friend, the river seemed like our friend, the pink rattlesnake eventually slithered away and we never saw our friend again.

We gathered water from the river and hung the bag from a tree to let the silt go to the bottom so we could filter it in the morning. Shufen couldn't stop talking about the pink rattlesnake, she was so excited.

I didn't know what to do, it was hot and I was covered in mud. I asked Shufen if it was okay if I walked around in my underwear, she said it was okay. I walked around in my underwear, it was nice to feel mostly naked six hours from civilization. I told Shufen she could take off her muddy clothes, but she didn't, she seemed extremely nervous about anything approaching sexuality. She later told me that her father had beaten her, that she felt scared most of her childhood, that sometimes when the noodles were not right, her father threw down his chopsticks and slapped her mother across the face right at the dinner table. That she had spent the first 20 years of her life living with the threat of violence breaking out at any moment. One time, she saw me drinking a beer, and she asked me if I was going to beat her. I told her no Shufen, not everyone beats women when they drink beer. I don't think she believed me. I didn't bother Shufen about her clothes, I smiled and told her I loved hiking with her, and that she is an amazing hiker. She always smiled when I told her she was a great hiker.

We sat together under the stars for a long time, we couldn't stop smiling, we didn't feel a sense of accomplish, we weren't the type of people that cared about accomplishments. I never heard Shufen ask how much money someone made or if they had a prestigious job, she didn't think about things like that. We were happy, because we were hikers, and we had in that moment, the perfect hike, we were hiking, we were sleeping in the wild, and we didn't want it to end.

We slept in a tiny tent together, we didn't touch, we slept with our backs to each other.

When we woke up in the morning, we put the tent together, filtered the water and packed the bags, and started off.

We started our walk, I carried the big pack on my back. We walked the wash, it was easy, it was basically flat with only a slight incline. We stopped by the four-inch creek and pumped more water, ate peanut butter and jelly sandwiches and kept marching on, there was little talking.

We eventually got to the incline, about the same time the sun came hot and began to beat us with its rays.

I kept walking ahead of Shufen, she got mad and yelled at me, "I'm alone, if I wanted to be alone, I do this by myself." I felt bad, and started to walk slow. At one point we were walking and Shufen was stepping up on a boulder and fell back, I saw her fall backwards, I ran back to help her, she was on the ground, lying on the rocks. Her face was red and flush, she was tired and hurting. I helped her up and gave her some water, she pretended to be strong, and kept walking.

We walked slowly, it wasn't gingerly, it was really slow. We became conscious of every step, we picked up one foot into the air, above the ground, and moved it a few inches forward. Then we picked another foot and moved it a couple of inches forward. We knew we had to walk it, we knew we had to keep moving, no one was on New Hance. On every other trail there were tourists, there were National Park Rangers patrolling the trails for sick hikers who might need assistance, but not New Hance Trail, there was not one footprint on that trail.

At one point, Shufen said from behind me, "Billy." I turned around and said, "Yes, Shufen."

Shufen replied, "I sleep." She put her pack down, lay on a flat rock and went to sleep. I lay down on the trail, put my pack behind my head as a pillow, closed my eyes and went to sleep too.

An hour later Shufen woke up and said, "Billy, wake up, we have to go."

We marched on.

I was exhausted, I couldn't think about anything anymore, a point had come where my thoughts had nothing left to give, no thoughts would come. I could no longer think about her and what happened in Korea, thoughts of Korea did not come at all. I no longer missed anyone, emotional pain did not come, only physical pain, my feet hurt, my legs hurt, and I wanted to eat two cheeseburgers and a pizza. When I looked back at Shufen, I could tell she was tired, but she was at peace, she knew the trail was safe, her father could not scare her deep in the Grand Canyon of North America.

The last mile was hard, we were covered in mud, sweat, and desert wind. We didn't smell good, our clothes were wrinkled, and our faces looked strained. But we made it the top, we did it, at the top, we fist bumped. It was obvious I was the first person to ever fist bump Shufen, but she did it, and she did it well.

We called for our friend to drive down and pick us up. As we sat there on the side of the road, Shufen told me that one day, she didn't know when, she would also hike the Andes of Peru, and the Pyrenees of Spain. She would have a long life of hiking. I believed her.

Time to Leave

It was September, getting colder every day. I lay in my bed wearing a hoodie and jeans. I was alone, I don't know what was wrong with me, but I decided to look at her Instagram. I wanted to look at her. I loved her face, I loved her little body. When we were dating, I would often look at her from across the room, we would be at a party, she would be on the other side of the living room talking to another person, I would be standing holding a beer, I would look at her, just talking, laughing and smiling, and be overcome with her beauty. I would keep talking to whoever was talking to me, but secretly I would be very passionate for her.

When we were in our tiny apartment in Korea, she would be cleaning or doing her makeup. I would watch her, admiring her, liking her movements, enjoying that someone was there, someone immensely enchanting, someone that made me feel so much.

I was alone in my dorm room at the Grand Canyon, she wasn't there. I wanted to look at her, I went to her Instagram, she had never removed the pictures from our relationship. I clicked on her Instagram, and there she was, she was at a party laughing, standing next to another man. He was laughing, she was laughing.

A terrible feeling flooded into me.

I had to leave North America, the continent was not big enough for the both of us. I contacted my friend David from Korea, he told me he was teaching English down in Santiago, Chile. He didn't get paid as much as we did in Korea, but it was enough to have an apartment, drink wine and eat. David told me he could get me a job if I just sent my resume. I sent David my resume, they hired me, they told me to get down there, they would fix up the work visa and get me in the classroom.

On my last night before I left, under the starry Grand Canyon sky I sat on a log outside drinking beer with Dream. We were wearing sweaters, coats and hiking shoes. Dream wasn't a nervous young man anymore, he was more confident after being in America for four months.

No one else was there, Kaja and Marcelina had left. When Kaja left I kissed her goodbye, she seemed sad. She mentioned to me that Poland had English schools, and she would help me get hired. I think she wanted me to love her, but I couldn't, few people will understand that. Most people, especially men, would call me the stupidest person alive, an amazing young woman wanted to love you, and what did you do? You moped around the Grand Canyon and went to Chile. I have no excuses, nothing I did at that time of my life made any sense. It was inexplicable even to me.

Dream said to me, "But why Chile? You could go to Montego Bay and hang out with me?"

"I have to find Pablo Neruda, Pablo Neruda knew about love, he loved someone. A woman sometimes loved him, but she decided to walk away from his love, and love someone else. Another man got all her best jokes, another man got to sleep next to her at night, another man held her hand in the park, another man grew old with her, and you know what hurts the most Dream?"

Dream looked worried, and said, "He gets to have sex with her?"

"No, that's not it. It is that she will be proud of the other man, when he accomplishes things, she will look into his eyes and tell him how proud of him she is. She never tells you again, 'I'm proud of you.' I just wanted that woman to be proud of me, but I could never do it. I never had her heart."

Dream said, "But you didn't want to live in Ohio, you didn't want that life, and she knew it. Look at you now, you are going to Chile, you obviously aren't done traveling."

"But I would have stayed there for her, I would have," I said pathetically.

"But that's not what you wanted, listen to what you're saying, 'would have,' it is obvious you didn't want to live there."

"If I don't want her, then why do I want her so much?"

Dream said," Because you feel like too many things have been taken, your brother died, your grandpa died, all your friends in Korea are gone, you don't relate to anyone in your hometown. You are putting all of your pain into her."

I sighed.

30 hours later I was sitting on the airplane flying to Chile. No one in that plane knew what pain lived inside me. At least in Chile I could pretend to be a happy person.

Epilogue

20 years later, the Grand Canyon was still the same. Even the South Rim remained the same. The El Tovar, Bright Angel and the Ice Cream Shack were still there. Millions of people were still visiting every year.

Early one summer morning, the woman Billy Cox once loved was sitting on the edge of the canyon, her 16-year-old daughter was sitting next to her, her husband was still in the hotel sleeping. She was staring at the canyon, loving it, holding a cup of coffee and smiling. She said out loud without thinking, "Billy loved this place."

Her daughter said surprised, laughing a little, "Who's Billy, mom?"

She had never told her daughter about Billy, the way veterans cannot speak of war to their children. To even think of Billy killed her, let alone to mention him, it would only lead to tears. He was there, when she was young and full of energy and hope for life, when everything seemed limitless. Her memories of him were always bathed in sunlight. Even when they took place in the snows of Ohio, they glowed with vibrance.

She spoke, "Before I met your dad, I loved a man named Billy. We met in college, then we went to Korea together for three years. We had so much fun. He was really a different kind of man. He had my heart, but certain things were done, certain things were said, and I just felt embarrassed. I couldn't get over my embarrassment. I was young, and thought things were bigger than they were. Your father knows this story, but we haven't mentioned it in years, so don't bring it up. After I broke up with Billy, he came out here to the Grand Canyon. Billy loved this canyon, he always told me how beautiful it was, he told me repeatedly that I needed to see it one day. Well, he came here and worked for the summer with a broken heart for me. When I was

153

young I was busy and didn't think about his broken heart. But now, I'm old enough to know, and feel, his broken heart."

She looked out at the canyon, she saw him, standing there with his back to her, a young, strong version of Billy. She saw him looking off into the canyon, with his mind dwelling on her, with his heart sore and bruised. She looked down at her body, it was young again, her skin was tight, her arms strong, she was wearing the clothes she bought in Korea with Billy. She looked at Billy on the edge, Billy turned around and looked at her, smiling. He nodded at her.

Noah Cicero is 38 years old and grew up in a small town near Youngstown, Ohio. He has lived in Eugene, Oregon, the Grand Canyon, Arizona, and Seoul, South Korea and currently resides in Las Vegas, Nevada. He has a movie made of his first book called *The Human War*, which won the 2014 Beloit Film Festival award for Best Screenplay. He has books translated into Turkish, Kurdish and Spanish. His first book of poetry *Bipolar Cowboy* was voted one of the best books on Goodreads in 2015. He has many short stories, articles and poems published at such places as Thought Catalog, 3AM Magazine, Wales Review and Amphibi.us.

neutralspaces.co/noahcicero

Made in the USA
San Bernardino, CA
07 November 2019